What do you love most about reading Harlequin Presents books? From what you tell us, it's our sexy foreign heroes, exciting and emotionally intense relationships, generous helpings of pure passion and glamorous international settings that bring you pleasure!

Welcome to February 2007's stunning selection of eight novels that bring you emotion, passion and excitement galore, as you are whisked around the world to meet men who make love in many languages. And you'll also find your favorite authors: Penny Jordan, Lucy Monroe, Kate Walker, Susan Stephens, Sandra Field, Carole Mortimer, Elizabeth Power and Anne McAllister.

Sit back and let us entertain you....

*Men who can't be tamed...or so they think!*

If you love strong, commanding men,
you'll love this miniseries.

Meet the guy who breaks the rules to get
exactly what he wants, because he is...

**HARD-EDGED & HANDSOME**
He's the man who's impossible to resist...

**RICH & RAKISH**
He's got everything—and needs nobody...
Until he meets one woman...

He's RUTHLESS!
In his pursuit of passion; in his world
the winner takes all!

Brought to you by your favorite
Harlequin Presents® authors!

# Lucy Monroe

## THE SICILIAN'S MARRIAGE ARRANGEMENT

TORONTO • NEW YORK • LONDON
AMSTERDAM • PARIS • SYDNEY • HAMBURG
STOCKHOLM • ATHENS • TOKYO • MILAN • MADRID
PRAGUE • WARSAW • BUDAPEST • AUCKLAND

ISBN-13: 978-0-373-12604-0
ISBN-10:  0-373-12604-2

THE SICILIAN'S MARRIAGE ARRANGEMENT

First North American Publication 2007.

Copyright © 2004 by Lucy Monroe.

www.eHarlequin.com

**Printed in U.S.A.**

All about the author...
*Lucy Monroe*

**LUCY MONROE** sold her first book in September
of 2002 to the Harlequin Presents line. That book
represented a dream that had been burning in her
heart for years: the dream to share her stories
with readers who love romance as much as she
does. Since then she has sold more than thirty
books to three publishers and hit national
bestseller lists in the U.S. and England, but since
selling that first book, the reader letters she
receives have touched her most deeply. Her most
important goal with every book is to touch a
reader's heart, and it is this connection that
makes those nights spent writing into the wee
hours worth it.

She started reading Harlequin Presents books very
young and discovered a heroic type of man
between the covers of those books—an honorable
man, capable of faithfulness and sacrifice for the
people he loves. Now married to what she terms
her "alpha male at the end of a book," Lucy believes
there is a lot more reality to the fantasy stories she
writes than most people give credit for. She believes
happy endings are really marvelous beginnings
and that's why she writes them. She hopes her
books help readers to believe a little, too...just like
romance did for her so many years ago.

Lucy enjoys hearing from readers and responds
to every e-mail. You can reach her by e-mailing
lucymonroe@lucymonroe.com

With thanks to Serena for her help with Italian phrases and perspective, but most of all for the warmth of her friendship!

# CHAPTER ONE

"HAVE you heard? He's trying to buy her a husband." Feminine laughter trilled mockingly.

"With his millions, it shouldn't be hard."

"The old man will live to see a hundred and five and keep control of his company right up until he dies," the woman said. "That means over thirty years married to a woman who is *hope*lessly introverted, *hope*lessly ordinary and probably *hope*less in bed, to boot. Practically a lifetime before her future husband will see any fruit for his labor."

"Put in that light," the man drawled sardonically, "the return on investment does seem pretty low."

"Why, darling, were you thinking of applying for the job?" Scornful disbelief laced the woman's too knowing voice.

The masculine laughter that came in reply grated on Luciano's nerves. He had arrived late to the New Year's Eve party hosted by the Boston based multi-millionaire, Joshua Reynolds. Nevertheless, he knew exactly whom the cynical woman and her male cohort were discussing: Hope Bishop—an extremely sweet and *sì*, very shy, young woman. She was also the granddaughter of their host.

Luciano hadn't realized the old man had decided to procure her a husband. It should come as no surprise. While she had the innocence of an eighteen-year-old, she must be twenty-three or four, having completed her degree at university two years ago. He remembered attending a formal dinner to celebrate.

The dinner, like any other social gathering hosted by Reynolds, had turned into a business discussion and the guest of honor had disappeared long before the evening was over. He had thought at the time he might be the only person to have noticed. Certainly her grandfather had not, nor had any of the other businessmen present remarked upon Hope's absence.

Luciano turned away from the gossiping couple and stepped around a potted plant easily as tall as most men. Its bushy foliage obstructed his view of what was behind it, which was why he didn't realize Hope Bishop was standing there in frozen mortification until he had all but stepped on her.

She gasped and moved backward, her corkscrew curls catching on the leaves behind her, their chestnut color a startling contrast to the plant's bright green shrubbery. "*Signor* di Valerio!"

He reached out to stop her from landing on her bottom in the big Chinese pot housing the plant.

Wide violet eyes blinked in attempt to dispel suspicious moisture. "Oh, I'm sorry. How clumsy I am."

"Not at all, *signorina*." The skin beneath his fingers was soft and warm. "I am the one who must apologize. I walked without looking ahead of myself and am at your feet in regret for my precipitous behavior."

As he had hoped it would, his overly formal, old-fashioned apology brought a small smile to tilt the generous lips that had a moment before been trembling. "You are very kind, *signor*."

She was one of the few people who believed this to be so. He let go of her arms, finding it surprisingly difficult to make his fingers release their captive. "And you are very lovely tonight."

It had been the wrong thing to say. Her gaze flitted to the shrub and the still gossiping couple beyond, her expression turning pained. Their voices carried quite clearly, now discussing an adulterous affair between two of their acquaintances. No doubt Hope had heard their earlier words.

She affirmed his thoughts when she softly said, "Not lovely, I think, but *hope*lessly average," telling him too that she knew he had heard the unflattering comments.

He did not like the sadness in her eyes and he once again took her arm, leading her toward the library. It was the one room unlikely to have a lot of New Year's Eve guests milling about. "Come, *piccola*."

Little one. It suited her.

She did not demur. That was one of the things he had always liked about the girl. She did not argue for the sake of it, not even with her overbearing and often neglectful grandfather. She was a peaceful sort of person.

They reached the library. He guided her inside, quickly ascertaining he had been right and no one else was present. He shut the door to keep it that way. She needed a few moments to collect herself.

Once again he was surprised by a desire to maintain his hold on her, but she tugged slightly on her arm and he released her. She faced him, her tiny stature accentuated by her three-inch heels, not diminished as he was sure she had hoped.

She really did look lovely in her formal gown of deep purple. The bodice outlined small, but perfectly proportioned curves while the shimmery fabric of the full skirt floated around her ankles in a very feminine way. She was not ravishingly sexy like the women he dated, but pretty in a very innocent and startlingly tantalizing way.

"I don't think he's trying to buy me a husband, you know." She tucked a reddish-brown curl behind her ear. "He's tried to buy me pretty much everything else since his heart attack, but I think even Grandfather would draw the line at buying a husband."

He wouldn't put anything past the wily old man, but forbore saying so. "It is natural for him to want to buy you things."

She grimaced. "Yes, I suppose so, but in the past he's always been impersonal with it."

A husband would be a pretty personal purchase, Luciano had to admit. "What do you mean, *signorina?*"

"Oh please, you must call me Hope. We've known each other for five years after all."

Had it been that long? "Hope then." He smiled and watched in some fascination as her skin took on a distinctly rosy hue.

She averted her face, so she was looking at the overfull bookcase on her left. "Grandfather has raised me since I was five."

"I did not know this."

She nodded. "But I don't think he noticed I even lived in his house except to instruct the servants to buy me what I needed, clothes when I grew out of them, books when I wanted them, an education, that sort of thing."

It was as he had always surmised. Hope had been

relegated to the background of Reynolds' life and she had known it.

"But just lately, he's been buying things for me himself. My birthday was a month ago and he bought me a car." She sounded shocked by the fact. "I mean he went to the car dealership and picked it out himself. The housekeeper told me."

"This bothers you?" Most women of his acquaintance would find a car a very appropriate birthday gift.

Her pansy eyes focused back on him. "No. Not really. Well, except that I don't drive, but that's not the point. It's just that I think he's trying to make up for something."

"Perhaps he regrets spending so little time with you through your formative years."

Her soft, feminine laughter affected his libido in a most unexpected way. "He had the housekeeper take me out to dinner for my birthday after having the Porsche delivered by the dealership."

"He bought you a Porsche?" That was hardly a suitable gift for a young woman who did not even know how to drive. *Porca miseria!* She could kill herself her first time behind the wheel with such a powerful car. He would have to speak to Reynolds about making sure she had received proper driving instruction before she was allowed onto the roads alone.

"Yes. He also bought me a mink coat. Not a fake one, but the real thing." She sighed and sat down in one of the burgundy leather reading chairs. "I'm, um…a vegetarian." She peeked up at him through her lashes. "The thought of killing animals makes me nauseous."

He shook his head and leaned back against the desk. "Your grandfather does not know you very well, does he, *piccola?*"

"I suppose not. I'm really excited about the six-week European tour he gave me for Christmas, though. Even if I won't be leaving for six months. He booked it for early summer." Her eyes shone with undisguised delight at the prospect. "I'll be traveling with a group of college students and a tour guide."

"How many other young women will there be?"

She shrugged. "I don't know. There will be ten of us in all, not including the guide of course." She crossed one leg over the other and started to swing the ankle back and forth, making her dress swish with each movement. "I don't know what the ratio of men to women will be."

"You are traveling with men?"

"Oh, yes. It's all coed. Something I would have loved to do in college, but better late than never, don't they say?"

He didn't know about that, but the idea of this naive creature spending six weeks with a group of libidinous, college age men did not please him. Why he should care, he did not stop to analyze. It was his nature to act on not only his behalf, but that of others as well.

"I do not think it is wise for you to go on such a trip. Surely a wholly female group would be more enjoyable for you."

Her leg stopped its swinging and she stared at him, clearly dumbfounded. "You're kidding, right? Half the reason for going on the trip is to spend some time with men close to my own age."

"Are you saying you object to Joshua buying you

a husband, but not when it comes to him buying you a lover?'' He didn't know what had made him say it. Only that he had been angry, an inexplicable reaction to the news she was interested in *male companionship*.

She blanched and sat back in her chair as if trying to put distance between them. ''I didn't say that. I'm not looking for a…a lover.'' Then in a whirl of purple chiffon, she jumped up. ''I'll just get back to the party.'' She eased around him toward the door as if he were an angry animal threatening to pounce.

He cursed himself in his native tongue as she opened the door and fled. There had been tears in her lavender eyes. What the gossiping duo had not been able to do with their nasty commentary, he had managed with one sentence.

He had made her cry.

Two now familiar hands grabbed her shoulders from behind. ''Please, *piccola,* you must allow me to once again apologize.''

She said nothing, but she didn't try to get away. How could she? The moment he touched her, she lost all sense of self-will. And he did not have a clue, but then why should he? Sicilian business tycoons did not look to hopelessly average, twenty-three-year-old virgins for an alliance…of any sort.

She blinked furiously at the wetness that had already trickled down to her cheeks. Wasn't it enough that she had been forced to overhear her shortcomings cataloged by two of her grandfather's guests? That Luciano of all people should have heard as well had increased the hurt exponentially. Then to have him accuse her of wanting her grandfather to buy her a lover! As if the idea that any man would desire her for herself was too impossible to contemplate.

"Let me go," she whispered. "I need to check on Grandfather."

"Joshua has an entire household of servants to see to his needs. I have only you."

"You don't *need* me."

He turned her to face him. Then keeping one restraining hand on her shoulder, he tipped her chin up with his forefinger. His eyes were dark with remorse. "I did not mean it, *piccola.*"

She just shook her head, not wanting to speak and betray how much his careless words had hurt. She was not blasé enough to take the type of sophisticated joking he had been indulging in with equanimity.

He said something low in Italian and wiped at her cheeks with a black silk handkerchief he had pulled from his pocket. "Do not distress yourself so. It was nothing more than a poorly worded jest. Not something for which you should upset yourself."

"I'm sorry. I'm being stupidly emotional."

His gorgeous brown eyes narrowed. "You are not stupid, *piccola,* merely easily hurt. You must learn to control this or others will take advantage of your weakness."

"I—"

"Consider… The words of that gossiping pair distressed you and yet you know them to be false. Your grandfather has no *need* to buy you either a husband or a lover." He accentuated his words with a small squeeze of her shoulder. "You are lovely and gentle, a woman any man would be lucky to claim."

Now she'd forced him to fabrication to get out of the sticky situation.

She made herself smile. "Thank you."

The stunning angles of his face relaxed in relief and he returned the smile.

Good. If she could convince him she was fine, he would let her leave and she could find someplace to lick her wounds in private.

No one else would notice if she disappeared from the party. Well, perhaps Edward, her colleague from the women's shelter would notice. Only she had left him thoroughly engrossed in a debate over archeological method with one of her grandfather's colleagues and doubted he would surface before the party ended.

She stepped back from Luciano's touch, as much out of self-preservation as her need to get away completely. His proximity affected her to a frightening degree.

"I'm sure there are other guests you would like to talk to." Again the small polite smile. "If you're anything like Grandfather, you see every social occasion as an opportunity to advance your business interests. Most of the guests are his business contacts."

"You are a poor prevaricator, Hope." He stepped toward her, invading her space with his presence and the scent of his expensive cologne. She wondered if he had it mixed especially for him because she'd never smelled anything as wonderful on another man.

"P-prevaricator?" she asked, stumbling over the word because he was so close.

"It means one who deviates from the truth." His mouth firmed with grim resolve that warned her she would not get away so easily. "Rather than discuss business with men I can see any day of the week, I would prefer you to show me to the buffet table. I came late and did not eat dinner tonight."

She'd already known he had come late. Actually, she had thought he was not coming at all. The first she had known of his arrival had been the debacle by the banana tree. "Then, by all means, allow me to show you to the food table."

It was her duty as hostess, after all.

She turned to lead the way and almost stopped in shock as she felt his hand rest lightly against her waist. By the time they reached the buffet, her emotions and heart rate were both chaotic.

"The food," she croaked out and waved her hand toward the table. ·

"Will you sit with me while I eat? I prefer not to do so alone."

What choice had she? To refuse would be churlish. "Yes, of course."

She stifled a sigh. She had thought he would let her escape once they arrived in the reception room of the old Boston mansion, but she'd been wrong. The only thing that equaled Sicilian revenge was Sicilian guilt. She wondered how much penance Luciano's guilt would require before he would feel comfortable relegating her to the background once more.

Usually, she would be rejoicing at the opportunity to spend time in his company. He had fascinated her since their first meeting five years ago. She had seen him two or three times a year since as he and her grandfather had many business interests in common. Even now, she found being the focus of his attention a heady experience, no matter that compassion and guilt were the reasons for it.

She waited until he had filled a plate and then led him to one of the many small duet tables surrounding the room. There were larger tables where someone else would undoubtedly join them, but selfishly she thought that if these few moments were all she would have of him, she wanted them private.

"Are you still working as a bookkeeper at the women's shelter?"

Surprised he had remembered, she said, "Yes. We're opening another facility outside of Boston in a few weeks."

He asked her about it and then spent the next twenty minutes listening to her talk about the women's shelter and the work they were doing. They catered to victims of domestic violence, but did a great deal for single mothers down on their luck as well. Hope loved her job and could talk about the shelter for hours.

"I suppose they can always use donations?" Luciano asked.

So, that was how he planned to finish mitigating his guilt for making her cry. Not that it was really his fault. He could not be blamed for her lack of urbanity, but she wouldn't refuse him regardless.

He had plenty of money to donate to such a worthy cause. He was so rich, he traveled with not simply a bodyguard, but a whole security team. The only reason he was alone now was because Grandfather's security was known to be some of the most stringent in the East Coast big business community.

"Yes. They bought the furniture for the upstairs with my fur coat, but there's still the downstairs to furnish."

He smiled and her insides did that imitation of melting Godiva chocolate they always did when those sensual lips curved in humor. "So, you sold the mink, hmm?"

"Oh no. That wouldn't be right. It was a gift after all. I gave it to the shelter." She winked and then felt herself blushing at her own temerity. "They sold it."

"You've got a streak of minx in you I think."

"Perhaps, *signor*. Perhaps."

"Do you have contact information for the shelter?"

"Naturally."

"I should like to give it to my P.A., and instruct that a donation large enough to furnish several rooms is made on my behalf."

"I've got a business card upstairs in my room, if you'll wait a moment while I get it?" What she would never do on her own behalf, she did for the shelter with total equanimity.

"I will wait."

Hope pulled a white business card for the women's shelter from the top drawer of the escritoire in the small study attached to her suite of rooms. As she turned to head back downstairs, she realized it was less than ten minutes before midnight. She stopped and stared at the ornamental desk clock, biting her lip. If she waited just a few minutes to return downstairs, she could avoid the ritual of kissing someone on the stroke of midnight.

She didn't fear being accosted by one of the many male guests at her grandfather's party. She was aware that the most likely scenario would be her standing alone and watching others kiss. Her stomach tightened at the thought of watching Luciano locking lips with some gorgeous woman. And there were plenty of them downstairs.

Rich businessmen attracted beautiful women who had a chic she envied and could not hope to emulate.

She wasn't worried about leaving Luciano to his own devices. Even now, she had no doubt he was no longer sitting alone while he waited for her. He might not even wait at the table, but expect her to come find him once she returned downstairs. Now that his guilt had been appeased, she would no longer qualify for his undivided attention.

Going back downstairs at this moment in time would serve no purpose other than to further underscore the humiliating fact that she did not fit amidst her grandfather's guests. She might have been born to his world, but she could never feel like she belonged in it. Perhaps because she had never felt like she belonged anywhere.

From the clock, her gaze shifted to the plaque hanging on the wall. It was a saying by Eleanor Roosevelt and it reminded her that she might not be able to help her shyness, but she did not have to be craven as well.

Luciano became aware of Hope instantly when she arrived once again in the periphery of his vision. She said and did nothing, but the sweet scent he associated with her reached out to surround him. He turned from the Scandinavian cover model who had approached him within seconds of Hope's disappearance from their table.

"You're back."

Her gaze flicked to the model and back to him. "Yes." She reached her hand out, a small white card between her delicate thumb and forefinger. "Here's the contact information for the shelter."

He took it and tucked it into the inner pocket of his formal dinner jacket. *"Grazie."*

"You're welcome."

Suddenly noisemakers started blaring around them and a ten second count down began in the other room. The model joined in as did the other guests surrounding him and Hope. Hope did as well, but an expression he did not understand crossed her features. Why should it make her sad to ring in the New Year?

He could not look away from the almost tragic apprehension turning her lavender eyes so dark, they appeared black. The blonde put her hand on his arm and he realized that men and women were pairing off. Ah, the traditional kiss to bring in the New Year with luck. And in a split second of clarity he understood Hope's sadness and that he had a choice. He could kiss the sexy, extremely world savvy woman to his left, or he could kiss Hope.

Her expression was carefully guarded, but he could tell that she expected him to kiss the model. She had grown accustomed to neglect and although she seemed more than willing to talk to him, she was terribly shy around others. She expected to kiss no one. And the expectation had put that sadness in her eyes. It was not right.

She was gentle and generous. What was the matter with the men of Boston that they overlooked this delicate but exotic bloom?

He shook off the blonde's hold and stepped toward Hope. Her eyes grew wide and her mouth stopped moving in the countdown, freezing in a perfect little *O*. Placing his hands on both sides of her face, he tilted it up for his kiss. A cacophony of *Ones* sounded around him and then he lowered his mouth to hers. He would kiss her gently, nothing too involved.

He did not want to frighten her, but he owed her

this small concession for having made her cry. Buying furniture for her women's shelter would not cut it. That was money, but the insult had been personal and this was personal atonement.

His lips touched hers and she trembled. He gently tasted her with his tongue. She was sweet and her lips were soft. They were still parted and he decided to go a step further. He wanted to taste the warmth and wetness of her mouth. So he did.

And it was good, better than he would have thought possible.

Her tongue tentatively brushed against his and heat surged through his male flesh. He wanted more, so he took it, moving one hand to her back and pressing her into him. She went completely pliant against him, molding her body to his like molten metal over a cast figure. Using the hand on her back, he lifted her off the floor until her face was even with his own and he could kiss her as urgently as he wanted to do.

She wrapped her arms around his neck and moaned, kissing him back with a passion that more than matched his own.

The small noises emanating from her drove him on.

He deepened the kiss further, oblivious now to his surroundings.

He wanted to do more than kiss her. He wanted to strip her naked and taste every centimeter of her delectable little body. The library. He could take her back to the library.

His hand was actually moving to catch her knees so he could carry her off when a booming voice broke through the daze of his lascivious thoughts.

"With a kiss like that, you're both bound to have more good luck than a Chinese dragon."

# CHAPTER TWO

LUCIANO'S head snapped up at the sound of Joshua Reynolds' humor-filled voice and reality came back with a painful thud. Hope was still clinging to him, her expression dazed, but the rest of the room was very much aware. And what they were aware of was that he'd been caught kissing the host's granddaughter like a horny teenager on his first date with an older woman.

He set Hope down with more speed than finesse, putting her away from him with a brusque movement.

She stared up at him, eyes darkened with passion and still unfocused. "Luciano?"

"Didn't know you two knew each other so well." A crafty expression entered Reynolds' eyes that Luciano did not like.

"It is not a requirement to know someone well to share a New Year's kiss," he replied firmly, wanting to immediately squelch any ideas the old man might have regarding Luciano and Hope as anything other than passing acquaintances.

"Is that right?" Reynolds turned to Hope. "What do you say, little girl?"

Hope stared at her grandfather as if she did not recognize him. Then her eyes sought out Luciano once again, the question in them making him defensive.

He frowned at her. "She is your granddaughter. You know as well as anyone how little I have seen of her over the years.'' His eyes willed Hope to snap out of her reverie and affirm his stand to her grandfather.

At first, she just looked confused, but then her expression seemed to transform with the speed of light. She went from dazed to hurt to horrified, but within a second she was doing her best to look unaffected.

It was not a completely successful effort with her generous lips swollen from the consuming kiss.

She forced a smile that hurt him to see because it was so obviously not the direction those lips wanted to go. ''It wasn't anything, Grandfather. Less than nothing.'' She spun on her heel without looking back at Luciano. ''I've got to check on the champagne.'' And she was gone.

He watched her go, feeling he should have handled that situation better and wishing he'd never come to the party in the first place.

''It didn't look like less than nothing to me, but I'm an old man. What do I know?''

The speculative tone of Joshua Reynolds' voice sent an arrow of wariness arcing through Luciano. He remembered the gossip he had overheard earlier. Rumors often started from a kernel of truth. The old man could forget trying to buy him as a husband for his shy granddaughter.

She might kiss with more passion than many women made love, but Luciano Ignazio di Valerio was not for sale.

He had no intention of marrying for years yet and when he did, it wouldn't be to an American woman with her culture's typically overinflated views on personal independence. He wanted a nice traditional Sicilian wife.

His family expected it.

Even if kissing Hope Bishop was as close to making love with his clothes on as he'd ever come.

Hope slammed the door of her bedroom behind her and then spun around to lock it for good measure.

It was after three o'clock and the last guest had finally departed. She'd made herself stay downstairs for the remainder of the party because she was guiltily aware her grandfather had arranged it for her benefit rather than business. He'd said as much when he told her he planned to have a New Year's Eve bash at the Boston mansion.

She wished he had not bothered. At least part of her did. The other part, the sensual woman that lurked inside her was reveling in her first taste of passion.

Luciano had kissed her. Like he meant it. She was fairly certain the whole thing had started as a pity kiss, but somewhere along the way, he'd actually gotten involved. So had she, but that was not so surprising.

She'd wanted to kiss the Sicilian tycoon for the better part of five years. It had been an impossible fantasy…until tonight. Then a combination of events had led to a kiss so devastating, it would haunt her dreams for years to come.

She plopped down onto the side of her bed and grabbed a throw pillow, hugging it to herself.

He had tasted wonderful.

Had felt hard and infinitely masculine against her.

Had smelled like the lover she desired above all others.

And then he had thrust her from him like a disease ridden rodent. She punched the cushion in her lap. He had been enjoying the kiss. She was sure of it, but then her grandfather had interrupted and Luciano had acted *embarrassed* to be caught kissing her.

Okay, maybe it did nothing for his sophisticated image to be caught taking pleasure in the kiss of an awkward twenty-three-year-old virgin who never dated. But surely it wasn't such a tragedy either. Not so bad that he had to shove her away like something he'd found under his shoe in a cow pasture.

The tears that had seemed to plague her for one reason or another all evening once again welled hot and stinging in her eyes. He'd made her look like a complete fool. She'd been forced to smile while cringing inside at the teasing and downright ribald comments tossed her way for the last three hours.

People were saying that she'd thrown herself at him. That he'd had to practically manhandle her to get her off of him. That as desperate spinsters went, she had won the golden cup.

Wetness splashed down her cheeks.

She'd heard it all while circulating among the guests. People had gone out of their way to speak loudly enough so she could not help overhearing. Some had made jokes to her face. A few of the male guests had offered to take on where Luciano had left off.

Grandfather remained blissfully ignorant, having closeted himself in the study with a businessman from Japan after the official New Year's toast. If she had anything to say about it, he would remain that way.

Luciano, the rat, had left the party within minutes of his humiliating rejection of her.

Even the joy of being kissed with such heady abandon by the one man she had ever wanted could not overshadow her degradation at his hands in front of a room filled with her grandfather's guests. She hated Luciano di Valerio. She really did.

She hoped she never saw him again.

"The shares are not for sale."

Luciano studied the man who had just spoken, looking for a chink in the old man's business armor, but Reynolds was a wily campaigner and not a speck of interest or emotion reflected in his gray eyes.

"I will pay you double what you gave my uncle for them." He'd already offered a fifty-percent return on investment. To no avail.

Reynolds shook his head. "I don't need more money."

The words were said with just enough emphasis to make a very pertinent point. Whatever Joshua Reynolds wanted in exchange for those shares, it wasn't money and he could afford to turn down Luciano's best offer.

"Then, *signor,* what is that you do need?" he asked, taking the bait.

"A husband for my granddaughter."

Impossible! *"Che cosa?"*

Joshua leaned back in his chair, his hands resting lightly on his oversize executive desk. "I'm getting on in years. I want to make sure I leave Hope taken care of. Regardless of what young women these days believe, and young men when it comes to it—that means seeing her married."

"I do not think your granddaughter would agree with you."

"Getting her to agree is your job. The girl doesn't know what is best for her. She spends all her free time working for the women's shelter, or the local animal shelter, or doing things like answering phones for the annual MDA telethon. She's a worse bleeding heart than her grandmother ever was.''

And it was unlikely she found the slightest understanding from the ruthless old bastard sitting across from Luciano. ''Are you saying that Hope doesn't know you're trying to buy her a husband?''

''I'm not interested in discussing what my granddaughter knows or doesn't know. If you want those shares, you're going to have to marry her to get them.''

The shares in question were for the original family-held Valerio Shipping, a company started by his great-grandfather and passed through each successive generation. While it rankled, having a nonfamily member holding a significant chunk of stock was not the end of the world.

He stood. ''Keep the shares. I am not for sale.''

''But Valerio Shipping is.''

The words stopped Luciano at the door. He turned. ''It is not. I would never countenance the sale of my family's company.'' Although his interests in Valerio Shipping represented a miniscule portion of his business holdings, his family pride would never allow him to offload it.

''You won't be able to stop me.''

''My uncle did not hold majority stock in the company.'' But the fool had sold the large block he *had* held to Joshua Reynolds rather than approach his nephew when gambling debts had made him desperate for cash.

''No, but with the proxy of some of your distant cousins as well as the stock I have procured from those willing to sell, I do control enough shares in the company to do what I damn well please with it.''

"I do not believe you." Many of those distant cousins had emigrated, but he could not believe they were so lost to family pride as to give an outsider their proxy or worse, sell their portion of Valerio Shipping to him.

His uncle he could almost believe. The man was addicted to wine, women and casinos. He had the self-discipline of a four-year-old and that was probably giving the man more credit than he deserved.

Reynolds tossed a report on the desk. "Read it.''

Luciano hid his mounting fury as he crossed the room and then lifted the report to read. He did not sit down, but flipped through the pages while still standing. Outraged pride grew with each successive page and coalesced into lava like fury when he read the final page.

It was a recommendation by Joshua Reynolds to merge with Valerio Shipping's number one competitor. If that were not bad enough, it was clear that while the other company would maintain their business identity, Valerio Shipping would cease to exist.

He tossed the report onto the gleaming surface of the walnut desk. "You are not trying to buy Hope a husband, you are trying to blackmail one.''

Reynolds shrugged broad shoulders, not even slightly stooped by his more than seventy years. "Call it what you like, but if you want to keep Valerio Shipping in the di Valerio family and operating business under the Valerio name, you will marry my granddaughter.''

"What is the matter with her that you have to resort to such tactics to get her a husband?''

For the first time since Luciano had entered the other man's office, Reynolds' guard dropped enough to let his reaction show. Luciano's question had surprised him.

It was in the widening of his eyes, the beetling of his steel gray brows. "There's nothing wrong with her. She's a little shy and a bleeding heart, I admit, but for all that she'll make a fine wife."

*"To a husband you have to blackmail into marriage?"*

In many ways, he was a traditional Sicilian male, but Joshua Reynolds made Luciano look like a modern New Man. Hope's grandfather was more than old-fashioned in his views. He was prehistoric.

"Don't tell me, you were waiting for love eternal to get married, man?" Derision laced Reynolds' voice. "You're thirty, not some young pup still dreaming of fairy tales and fantasies. And you're plenty old enough to be thinking about a wife and family. Your own father is gone, so cannot advise you, but I'm here to tell you, you don't want to leave it too late to enjoy the benefits of family life."

Not only did Luciano find the very idea of taking advice from a man trying to blackmail him offensive, but Joshua Reynolds was the last person to hand out platitudes about enjoying family life. He'd spent his seventy plus years almost completely oblivious to his own family.

"I'm offering you a straightforward business deal. Take it or leave it." The tone of Reynolds' voice left no doubt how seriously he felt about following through on his threats.

"And if I leave it my family company ceases to exist."

The other man looked unconcerned by the reminder. "No company lasts forever."

Gritting his teeth, Luciano forced himself not to take the other man by the throat and shake him. He never lost control and he would not give his adversary the benefit of doing so now.

"I will have to think about it."

"You do that and think about this while you are at it. My granddaughter left two weeks ago for a tour of Europe in the company of four other girls, a tour guide and five young men. Her last letter mentioned one of them several times. David something or other. Apparently, they are developing quite the friendship. If you want Hope to come to the marriage bed untouched, you'd better do something about it soon."

Hope peered through the viewer of her state-of-the-art digital camera that had been a parting gift from her grandfather before her trip. She knelt down on one knee, seeking the perfect shot of the Parthenon in the distance. The waning evening light cast the ancient structure in purplish shadows she had been determined to catch on disc.

It was a fantastic sight.

"It's going to be dark before you get the shot, Hope. *Come on, honey, take your picture already.*" David's Texas drawl intruded on her concentration, making her lose the shot she'd been about to snap and it was all she could do not to ask him to take himself off.

He'd been so nice to her over the past three weeks, offering her friendship and a male escort when circumstances required it. She'd been surprised how at ease she'd felt with the group right off, but a lifetime of shyness did not dissipate overnight. Feeling comfortable had not instantly translated into her making overtures of friendship. David had approached her, his extroverted confidence and easy smile drawing her out of her shell.

Because of that, she forced back a pithy reply, despite her surge of unaccustomed impatience. "I'll just be a second. Why don't you wait for me back at the bus?"

"I can't leave my best girl all by herself. Just hurry it up, honey."

She adjusted the focus of her camera and snapped off a series of shots, then stood. Interruptions and all, she thought the pictures were going to turn out pretty well and she smiled with satisfaction.

Turning to David, she let that smile include him. "There. All done." She closed the shutter before sliding her camera into its slim black case and then she tucked that into her oversize shoulder bag.

"Okay, we can return to the bus now." She couldn't keep the regret from sliding into her voice. She didn't want to leave.

David shook his head. "We're not scheduled to go back to the hotel for another twenty minutes."

"Then why were you rushing me?" she demanded with some exasperation.

His even white teeth slashed in an engaging grin. "I wanted your attention."

She eyed the blond Texan giant askance. In some ways he reminded her of a little boy, mostly kind but with the self-centeredness of youth. "Why?"

"I thought we could go for a walk." He put his hand out for her to take, clearly assuming her acquiescence to his plan.

After only a slight hesitation, she took it and let him lead her away from the others. A walk *was* a good idea. It was their last day in Athens and she wanted this final opportunity to soak in the ambience of the Parthenon.

David's grip on her hand was a little tight and she wiggled her fingers until he relaxed his. She was unused to physical affection in any sense and it had taken her a while to grow accustomed to David's casual touching. In some ways, she still wasn't. It helped knowing that he wasn't being overly familiar, just a typical Texas male—right down to his calling her honey as often as he used her name.

She stopped and stared in awe at a particularly entrancing view of the ancient structure. "It's so amazing."

David smiled down at her. "Seeing it through your eyes is more fun than experiencing it myself. You're a sweet little thing, Hope."

She laughed. "What does that make you, a sweet *big* thing?"

"Men aren't sweet. Didn't your daddy teach you anything?"

She shrugged, not wanting to admit she couldn't even remember her father. She only knew what he looked like because of the pictures of her parents' wedding her grandfather had on display in the drawing room. The framed photos showed two smiling people whom she had had trouble identifying with as her own flesh and blood.

"I stand corrected," she said. "I won't call you sweet ever again, but am I allowed to think it?"

The easy banter continued and they were both laughing when they returned to the tour bus fifteen minutes later, their clasped hands swinging between them.

"Hope!"

She looked away from David at the sound of her name being called. The tour operator was standing near the open door of the bus. She waved at Hope to come over. A tall man in a business suit stood beside her, dwarfing her with his huge frame. The growing darkness made it difficult to discern his features and Hope could not at first identify him. However, when he moved, she had a moment of blindingly sure recognition.

No one moved like Luciano di Valerio except the man himself. He had always reminded her of a jaguar she'd once seen in a nature special when she was an adolescent, all sleek, dark predatory male.

David stopped when they were still several yards from the bus, pulling her to a halt beside him. "Is that someone you know?"

Surprised by the aggressive tone in her friend's voice, she said, "Yes. He's a business associate of my grandfather's."

"He looks more like a *don* in the Mafia to me."

"Well, he *is* Sicilian," she teased, "but he's a tycoon, not a loan shark."

"Is there a difference?" David asked.

She didn't get a chance to reply because Luciano had started walking toward them the moment David stopped and he arrived at her side just as David finished speaking. Regardless of her wish to never see the man again, her eyes hungrily took in every detail of his face, the strong squarish jaw, the enigmatic expression in his dark brown eyes and the straight line of his sensual lips.

"I have come to take you to dinner," he said without preamble or indeed even the semblance of having asked a question.

"But how in the world did you come to be here?" Bewilderment at seeing him in such a setting temporarily eclipsed her anger toward him.

"Your grandfather knew I would be in Athens. He asked me to check on you."

"Oh." Ridiculously deflated by the knowledge he was there under her grandfather's aegis rather than his own, she didn't immediately know what else to say.

David had no such reticence. "She's fine."

The comment reminding her of not only his presence, but her manners as well. "Luciano, this is David Holton. David, meet Luciano di Valerio."

Neither man seemed inclined to acknowledge the introduction.

David eyed Luciano suspiciously while the tycoon's gaze settled on their clasped hands with unconcealed displeasure. Then those dark eyes were fixed on her and the expression in them was not pleasant. "I see you have decided to go for option two after all."

At first, she couldn't think what he meant and then their conversation in the library came back to her. Option one had been a husband, she supposed. Which meant that option two was a lover. He was implying she and David were lovers.

Feeling both wary and guilty for no reason she could discern, she snatched her hand from David's. "It's not like that," she said defensively before coming to the belated conclusion it wasn't his concern regardless.

David glared down at her as if she'd mortally offended him when she let go of his hand. "I planned to take you out this evening."

"I am sorry your plans will have to be postponed," Luciano said, sounding anything but. He inclined his head to her. "I have apprised your tour guide that I will return you to your hotel this evening."

"How nice, but a bit precipitous." She didn't bother to smile to soften the upcoming rejection. After the way he had treated her at the New Year's Eve party, he didn't deserve that kind of consideration. "It was kind of Grandfather to be concerned, but there is no need for you to give up your entire evening in what amounts to an unnecessary favor to him."

"I agreed to check on you for your grandfather's sake. I wish to spend the evening with you for my own."

She couldn't believe what she was hearing. *She refused to believe it.* She glared helplessly at him. Six months ago, he had kissed her to within an inch of her life, then thrust her away as if she were contaminated. He'd left her to face hours of humiliating comments and loudly spoken asides. *And*…she hadn't heard word one from him in all the intervening months.

David moved so that his body blocked her view of Luciano. "I thought I would take you to that restaurant you liked so much our first day here, honey." The accusation in his voice implied he had exclusive rights to her time, not to mention the altogether unfamiliar inflection he gave the word *honey*.

Nothing could be further from the truth.

"You could have said something earlier," she censored him.

"I wanted it to be a surprise," he responded sullenly. "I didn't expect some arrogant Italian guy to show up and try to spirit you away."

The situation was getting more unreal by the minute. Men never noticed her and yet here were two battling for her company.

She was tempted to tell Luciano to take a flying leap, but part of her also wanted a chance to rake him over the coals for his callous treatment of her. An insidious curiosity about why he wanted to be with her after rejecting her so completely was also niggling at her.

It would probably be downright brainless to give in to that curiosity or her desire to get a little of her own back, however. She had the awful feeling that her stupidly impressionable heart would be only too ready to start pining for him again if she allowed herself the luxury of his company.

*When did you stop pining for him? Was that before or after the ten times a day you forget what you're doing remembering how it felt to be kissed by him?* She ignored the mocking voice of her conscience, infinitely glad mind reading was not one of Luciano's many accomplishments.

Going with Luciano would not be a bright move.

On the other hand, she was uncomfortable with the proprietary attitude David was exhibiting. It struck her suddenly that he'd been growing increasingly possessive of her time over the past days. She hadn't minded because it meant she didn't have to put herself forward in unfamiliar situations, but they were just friends. It bothered her that he thought he could plan her time without her input.

She chewed her bottom lip, unsure what to do.

She felt wedged between two unpleasant alternatives, neither of which was going to leave her unscathed at the end of the evening.

# CHAPTER THREE

"OUR reservations are for eight-thirty. We have to be on our way, *piccola mia*," Luciano said, completely ignoring David.

"Are all European men so arrogant?" David asked her in direct retaliation.

She shot a quick sideways glance to see how Luciano had taken her friend's insolence. His expression was unreadable. "Shall we go?" he asked her.

David expelled an angry hiss.

She laid her hand on his forearm. This was getting ridiculous and if she didn't act soon, her friend would be well on his way to making an enemy of a very powerful man. David was too young to realize the long term impact on his future business dealings such an action might have. Though she was irritated by David's behavior, she liked him too much to let him do something so stupid.

Besides, if she went with Luciano, she hoped David would get the message she wanted his friendship, but wasn't interested in anything more. She couldn't be. She might want to hate Luciano, but he remained the only man she could think of in that way.

She had no experience with brushing off a man's interest and this seemed the easiest way.

"I'm sorry. Can we make it another night?" she asked by way of atonement.

"We won't be in Athens another night," he reminded her.

"I know."

He would probably have said more, but the bus driver called the final boarding call, shouting specifically for David to get a move on.

"You'd better go," she said, relieved the confrontation could not be prolonged. "I'll see you tomorrow."

"All right, honey." He bent down and kissed her briefly on the lips.

Shocked, she stared at him speechless. He'd never even kissed her cheek before.

He smiled, not with his usual friendly grin, but with an implied intimacy that did not exist between them. "If you don't want to wait for morning, you can come by my room tonight after your grandfather's crony drops you off."

The implication that Luciano was old enough to be in her grandfather's generation was enough to make her lips quirk despite the unwelcome kiss and male posturing.

"Perhaps your young friend's dates are used to going home unsatisfied and in need of further male companionship," Luciano drawled silkily, "but I can promise you, *bella mia,* you will have no such need tonight."

She gasped, all humor fleeing, and glowered at both men. "That's enough. *Both of you.* I have no intention of letting anyone *satisfy* me." She blushed even as she said the words and was irritated with herself for doing so.

"I do not appreciate this petty male posturing either." She didn't have to choose the best of two poor options, she could make another one. "I don't think I want to have dinner out at all. I'd rather eat room service alone in my hotel room than be in the company of *any* arrogant male."

With a triumphant glare at Luciano that did not endear him to her, David loped off toward the bus where the driver stood at the open door with obvious impatience. She started to follow him, determined to do just as she'd threatened. David might think he'd won, but he would find out differently if he tried to coax her out of her room tonight.

She'd gotten no further than a step when Luciano's hands settled on her shoulder, arresting her in midflight. "We need to discuss your regrettable tendency to leave before our conversations are finished. It is not polite, *piccola*."

He pulled her into his side and waved the bus driver off in one fluid movement.

She watched in impotent anger as the big vehicle pulled away. It was that, or scream like a madwoman for the bus driver to stop. She wasn't even sure he would hear her with the door closed and the rather noisy air-conditioning unit running full tilt. And she had absolutely no desire to make a spectacle of herself in front of the tourists milling about the parking area. His highhanded tactics had effectively left her with no choice but to stay behind with Luciano.

She didn't have to like it however and she tore away from his side with unconcealed contempt. "That was extremely discourteous, *signor*. I don't appreciate being manhandled, nor do I accept you have the right or the reason to dictate my activities."

He frowned down at her. "I may not yet have the right, but I do have the reason. I wish to spend time with you, *cara*."

"And my wishes count for nothing?" she de-

manded while reeling inside from such an admission
from him as well as the tender endearment.

"Your wishes are of utmost importance to me, but
do you really prefer ordering room service to an evening spent in my company?"

That was very much in question. It wasn't her preference, but her preservation she was concerned about.
"You were insufferably rude. You implied you were
going to… That we… As if I would!"

She could not make herself say the words aloud
and that made her mad. Angry with him for implying
he was going to take her to bed in the first place and
furious with herself for still being such a backward
creature she couldn't discuss sex without blushing
like the virgin she was.

His laughter was the last straw as far as she was
concerned. She didn't have to stick around to be made
fun of. She'd suffered enough at his hands in that
regard already.

She turned on her heel with every intention of finding some sort of public transport to take her back to
the hotel. Once again he stopped her. This time, he
wrapped his arms around her middle and pulled her
back into his body with a ruthless purpose.

His lips landed on her nape in a sensual caress that
sent her thoughts scattering to the four winds. "I have
ached to taste you again for six long months. You
must forgive me if my enthusiasm for your company
makes me act without proper courtesy."

Enthusiasm did not take six months to act, but she
was too busy trying not to melt into a puddle of feminine need at his feet to tell him so. "Luciano?" she
finally got out.

He spun her around to face him. "Spend the evening with me, *cara*. You know you want to."

"David was right. You are arrogant."

"I am also right."

She would have argued, but he kissed her. The moment his lips touched hers, she was lost. His mouth moved on hers with expert effect, drawing forth a response she could not hide or control. She allowed his tongue inside her mouth after the first gentle pressure applied to the seam of her lips.

He tasted like she remembered. Hot. Spicy. Masculine.

When he pulled away, she was too lost in her own sensual reaction to his kiss to even notice he was leading her anywhere. It wasn't until he stopped at the waiting limo and rapped out instructions to the ever-present security team, that she once again became aware of her surroundings.

Mary, mother of Joseph, it was just like at the party.

He could have done anything to her and she would have let him. She was also aware that while she'd been completely lost to reality, he had been in absolute control.

She tried to tell herself she was letting him hand her into the car because she didn't relish riding public transport alone at night in a foreign country. But she knew the truth. If she didn't sit down soon, she'd fall down. Her legs were like jelly and no way did she want him realizing that betraying fact.

Inside the car, she fiddled nervously with the strap of her brightly colored shoulder bag. It had a pattern of bright yellow and orange sunflowers all over it. She'd bought it so that it would be easily spotted among the other ladies' bags on the tour, but it looked gauche sitting on the cool leather seat of the ultra-luxurious limo.

She was also positive that her casual lemon yellow sundress and flat leather sandals were not *de rigueur* for the types of restaurants he frequented.

"I think it would be best if you took me back to my hotel," she said at the same time as he asked, "Are you enjoying your holiday?"

Her eyes met Luciano's in the well-lit interior of the car. Apparently neither one of them wanted to discuss the recent kiss.

His intense gaze mesmerized her. "I do not wish to take you back to your hotel."

"I'm not dressed for dinner out." She indicated her casual, day worn clothes with a wave of her hand.

"You look fine."

She snorted in disbelief. "Where are we eating, a hot dog stand?"

"I do not think they have those in Athens, *cara.*"

"You know what I mean."

She didn't even want to think how her hair looked. She'd long ago given up trying for a chic hairstyle and wore her natural curls in an only slightly tamed riot. Most of the time it suited her, but she could imagine that after spending the day tramping the streets of Athens it probably looked like she'd never brushed her hair in her life.

"You must trust me, *piccola.* I would not embarrass you."

That was rich, coming from him.

"Now, please, won't you tell me how you are finding your holiday? I remember you looked forward to it very much."

He had closed the privacy window between them and the front seat and turned on the tiny lights that ran the entire length of the roof, giving off a surprisingly illuminating glow. A glow that cast his features in stark relief. The genuine interest reflected in his expression prompted her to answer.

"It's been wonderful."

"And what has been your favorite stop so far?"

She couldn't believe a man of his extensive experiences would truly be interested in her first taste of Europe, but she answered nonetheless. "I really can't say." She smiled, remembering all the incredible things she'd seen. "I've loved every moment. Well, maybe not the airports, but David and the others have made the waiting around in drab terminals fun."

Luciano frowned at the mention of David's name. "It is not serious between you two?"

"If it were, you put a spanner in the works tonight, didn't you?" She might have preferred that spanner, but he didn't know that and his behavior had been unreasonable.

He did not look in the least bit guilty. "He implied you might come back to his room tonight. Are you sleeping with him?"

"That's none of your business!"

He leaned over her, the big torso of his six feet, four inch body intimidating at such close range. Suddenly he didn't remind her of just any old jaguar, but a hungry one intent on hunting his prey and moving in for the kill.

She felt like the prey.

"Tell me."

She was shy, but she wasn't a coward, or so she reminded herself frequently. "No. And if you're going to act like some kind of Neanderthal brute all evening, you may as well tell your chauffeur to take me back to my hotel right now."

She'd said it so many times now, it was beginning to sound like an impotent litany.

Amazingly, he backed off. Physically anyway.

"I am no brute, but I admit the thought you share your body with him does not predispose me to good temper."

"Why?"

"Surely after the kiss we shared only minutes ago, you do not have to ask this."

"Are you saying you give the third degree to every woman you kiss?" She didn't believe it.

"You are not every woman."

"No. I'm the hopelessly introverted, hopelessly average and probably hopeless in bed granddaughter of your business associate." The bitter memory rolled off her tongue before she became conscious what the word *probably* would reveal to him. Maybe he wouldn't notice she'd all but told him she was not sleeping with David. "I don't see where that makes me anything special to you."

It seemed he hadn't comprehended the implication of her words when he spoke. "You are not introverted with this David fellow. You were laughing with him and holding his hand."

He made it sound like she'd been caught *in flagrante delicto* with David. "He's my friend."

"I also am your friend, but you do not hold my hand."

"For Heaven's sake, you wouldn't hold a woman's hand unless it was to lead her to bed." Had she really said that?

"And are you trying to say this is not where your *friend* David was leading you?"

"Don't be ridiculous!"

"It is not ridiculous for me to think this. He looks at you with the eyes of a man who has claim to you."

"There is such thing as the claim of friendship."

·   "And friendship requires late night visits to his hotel room?"   ·

"I've never been to his hotel room late at night, for goodness' sake. I'm hardly the type to carry on a brief affair, or did you miss the hopeless-in-bed description?" As the words left her mouth, she realized with chagrin she'd given Luciano what he wanted— a definite answer to whether or not she was sleeping with David.

He didn't look smug, however. He was too busy glaring at her. "Stop repeating that bitch's words as if they are gospel. She knows nothing of you or your passions. You will be a consuming fire in my bed, of that I am certain."

*"Your bed?"*

He sighed. "I have no plans to seduce you tonight, so you can relax."

*"But you do plan to seduce me?"* She pinched the inside of her elbow to make sure she was not sleeping and having some bizarre dream. Pain radiated to her wrist. She was awake.

"Perhaps you will care to tell me what restaurant so caught your approval on your first day in the city?" he asked, ignoring her question.

Certain she'd had all the seduction talk she could take for one night, she eagerly accepted his change of subject. She told him about their visit to the night-life of the Psiri where she'd sampled out of this world food at one of the many small cafés that did not even open until six in the evening.

"It was a lot like Soho, but I felt more comfortable in Psiri than I ever did visiting that section of New York City. Maybe that's because I went there with my roommate from college. She was from Manhattan and her friends were all very gothic." Hope could still remember how out of place she'd felt in the avant garde atmosphere.

"Psiri is fantastic and a lot more laid back. I didn't feel like I was on display, if that makes any sense." Her Boston manners and introverted ways had made her feel out of place in Soho, but the Psiri was patronized by so many different nationalities, no one person stood out.

Luciano shrugged, his broad shoulders moving fluidly in the typical European movement. "I have never been to Soho and it has been several years since I indulged in the nightlife of Athens."

"I suppose it's hard to do normal things like drink ouzo in a small bar on a busy street when you've got a security team trailing you." Like the one in the nondescript car behind the limousine.

"*Sì*, and there is the lack of time as well. I have spent the better part of the last ten years building my business holdings. My socializing has been of necessity targeted to that end."

"Just like Grandfather."

"Perhaps."

"Is that what tonight is about? Are you doing my grandfather a favor in return for which you are angling for some kind of business coup?"

Luciano went curiously still. "What makes you ask this?"

It was her turn to shrug. "I don't know. I guess it's just hard to believe you've thought about me at all over the past six months." She ignored his threatened intent to seduce her as macho posturing. It must be a Sicilian male thing. "It's not as if you'd called or anything. And I know I'm not your average date."

He might socialize for business, but the companions he chose to do it with were invariably gorgeous and terribly sophisticated. Much like the model he had turned away from on New Year's Eve to kiss Hope instead. She still found that inexplicable. One of his previous *amours* had been a dispossessed princess with a reputation for fast living. His latest was an Italian supermodel who gave sultry new meaning.

Hope was as far from such a being as Luciano was from an awkward teenager.

"Accept that it pleases me to see you."

"Why should I?"

"Because I say it is so." Exasperation laced his every word and she wanted to kick him.

"You can say anything, but it's your actions that show what you really feel."

"What is that supposed to mean?"

Their arrival at their destination prevented further conversation.

Luciano helped Hope out of the limousine. Who would believe such a shy little thing could be such a termagant as well? After her response to his kiss on New Year's Eve, he had been sure wooing her would be the easy part of the deal with Joshua Reynolds. However, she was hardly falling into his arms in gratitude for his pursuit.

By the saints, she was contrary. She melted against

him when he took her in his arms, but she had the tongue of an asp.

That tongue was silent during the elevator ride to his Athens penthouse. She kept her gaze averted too. He wondered at this. He wondered also if she was enamored of that blond buffoon who had put his lips on her. A definite rapport existed between them. She said she did not sleep with him, but it was not because the man was averse. Anger still simmered beneath the surface at the memory of another man touching the woman who was to be his.

That she did not yet realize she belonged to Luciano was the only reason he had not flattened the American, but soon both she and he would know it. And then let the blond man touch her at his peril.

The elevator stopped and Hope looked up for the first time. "Where are we?"

The doors slid open and he stood back for her exit first. "This is my Athens headquarters."

They stepped through one of the two doors on the landing.

She looked around them. "It looks more like a home to me, or are you trying to tell me that a Sicilian tycoon does his business in the living room rather than the boardroom?"

He felt his lips quirk at her sassiness. This unexpected side to her nature was not altogether unpleasing. A wife without spirit would not suit him. He had yet to decide if he would let the marriage stand once he had his plans for dealing with her grandfather in place.

"The apartment is located on the top floor of the Valerio building. My office is one floor below."

If Hope was ignorant of the old man's machinations, her only guilt was by association. Tradition dictated the family held responsibility for the actions of one, but he was not such a dinosaur. If she knew nothing, he could not honorably include her in the vendetta and the marriage would have to stand.

"And the other door?" she asked.

"A company apartment."

Her brow quirked. "Not the home of your mistress?"

*Ai, ai, ai.* "You are a spitting kitten tonight."

She blushed and once again turned her face away from him.

He had brought her with him tonight to determine the level of her guilt as much as to woo her to marriage. Her ongoing contrariness was a point in favor of her innocence. Surely if she wanted the marriage and were in league with her grandfather, she would not be so difficult toward Luciano.

On the other hand, women had known since time memorial that to play hard to get intrigued the hunter in men, particularly Sicilian men.

"I thought you were taking me out to dinner. You said our reservations were for eight."

"And so they are. My chef has prepared a special meal to be served on the terrace. If we were late, sauces would be ruined, the vegetables overcooked."

She turned, her composure restored. "What a tragedy," she said facetiously.

"*Sì.* A great tragedy."

"We're eating on the terrace?"

"It has a magnificent view of the city. I believe you will like it."

The violet of her eyes mirrored confusion. "Why are you doing this? You can't be so hard up for a date that you must spend the evening with your business associate's granddaughter.''

"I told you, it pleases me. Why do you find this so difficult to believe?" He was not used to having his word questioned and he found he did not like it, especially from her.

She made a sound of disbelief. ''You date supermodels, sexy, sophisticated women. *I'm not your type.*''

For some reason her protestations on that point irritated him immensely. "A man will taste many types of fruit before finding a tree he wishes to eat from for a lifetime.''

"So, you're saying you were in the mood for an apple or something instead of the more exotic fruits?" The prospect did not appear to please her.

He stepped forward until their bodies were only inches apart and reached out to cup her face. "Perhaps you are the tree that will satisfy me for a lifetime.''

Hope felt herself go absolutely rigid in shock. She even stopped breathing. Her, the tree that could satisfy him for a lifetime? It was inconceivable, but why had he said it?

His hands dropped away from her face and he stepped back, giving her room to breathe. ''Would you like to freshen up before dinner?''

Sucking air into her oxygen-starved lungs, she nodded. Anything to get away from his enervating presence. He led her to a guest room and stood aside for her to enter. She could see an en suite off to the left.

She paused in the doorway without looking at him. ''Please don't play with me, Luciano. I'm not in your league." She didn't want to be hurt again like she had been on New Year's Eve. She didn't want to be just another fruit for his jaded palate.

Once again his hands were on her and he turned her to face him. She met his eyes, her own serious. He ran his fingertip over her bottom lip and her whole body trembled.

"I am not playing, *cara.*"

She so desperately wanted to believe him, but the memory of New Year's Eve was still too fresh. "Why..." She found she could not force the rest of the question past the lump of hope and wariness in her throat.

"Why what?"

"Why did you shove me away like a disease-ridden rodent after our kiss on New Year's Eve?" The words tumbled out with all the pain and rejection she had felt that night six months ago.

He looked outraged. "I did not do this."

"Excuse me, you did. I was there."

"I too was there. Perhaps I let you go a trifle quickly. I did not wish to embarrass you with further intimacies."

*"You didn't want to embarrass me?"* The irony of such an excuse was too great to be born. "I don't believe it."

"Believe."

"So, to save me embarrassment, you chose to humiliate me instead?" she asked in incredulity. If that was how the male mind worked, no wonder women had such a hard time understanding them.

"To kiss Luciano di Valerio is not a humiliation."

*"But to be publicly rejected by you is!"*

# CHAPTER FOUR

A MUSCLE ticked in his jaw. "Explain."

She was only too happy to do so. "I spent three hours as the butt of every joke in the room. Poor *hopeless* Hope, throwing herself at the gorgeous Italian," she mimicked with savage pain. "*Did you see how he had to practically tear her arms off of him? We always knew she was hopeless,* but to be that *desperate.*"

The cruel voices echoed in her head as if it had just happened and the painful mortification sliced her heart.

"This cannot be true. *I* kissed *you*. Surely the other guests saw that. *Porca miseria!* I rejected that tall blonde's advances to do it."

"Oh, yes, the model." Hope's body went taut with remembered emotion. "You know that old saying about a woman scorned? Well, she epitomized it. She told anyone who would listen that I pushed her out of the way to get to you."

Without the model's interference, Luciano's rejection would have remained a personal source of pain, not become a public humiliation.

"What is her name?" The chill in his voice surprised Hope.

"What difference does it make?" Did he think he could do something about it at this late date? The time for his action on her behalf was past. "Anyway, I don't know her name. I just hope I never see her

again. I wish I never had to see any of them again.''
Impossible when so many of the party guests had
been her grandfather's business associates and she often acted as his social hostess, albeit a quiet one.

He swore in Italian. She didn't recognize the word,
but she knew that tone. It was the same one her grandfather reserved for certain four-letter words.

''Do you know how many of the male guests offered to give me what you supposedly wouldn't?'' she
asked in driven tones. ''Strictly as an act of charity,
mind you.''

As if no man would ever *want* her enough to go
after her. Well, David wanted her. He'd told her she
could come to his room tonight. Maybe she would.
At least he wouldn't think he was doing her some
kind of favor.

''I want the names of these men.'' The rage in him
was a palpable force and quite frightening.

She stepped back from him. ''Why?''

''They insulted you.'' He said it as if those three
words should explain everything.

They didn't. ''So did you.''

''Tell me their names.'' He totally ignored his own
culpability, but the deadly tone of his voice indicated
he was far from ignoring the insult offered to her by
the other guests.

Why was he taking this so personally?

''I don't think I should.''

''Nevertheless, you will.''

''Don't try to boss me around, Luciano.'' She
would have sounded a lot more convincing if her
voice hadn't broken on his name, but suddenly he was
looming too close and she felt way more intimidated
than she wanted to.

"I am a bossy guy by nature, ask my sister. It is something you will have to get used to, *cara*."

"I don't think so."

"I want the names of the men who made importunate remarks to you."

"There really weren't that many." Two to be exact, but at the time it had definitely been two too many.

"So recalling their names should not be a difficulty, *sì?*"

She sighed. "What are you going to do if I tell you?"

"I will have words with them."

"That's all? Just words."

His expression was unreadable. "Just words."

She named the two men who had gone out of their way to be so objectionable. One had even trapped her in the hallway and kissed her. After Luciano's kiss, any other man's mouth was a repugnance and she had kicked him in the shin, leaving him hopping on one leg and cursing her.

"You must believe I did not intend such a thing to happen."

"I know." At least she did now. His shock and rage were too real. "However, you have got to see that it would be better for me if you just left me alone. I know I'm introverted and my looks are nothing to speak of, but I'm a woman with feelings and I don't want to be hurt any more."

And he was the only man with the real power to hurt her. The others had caused her embarrassment, but Luciano's rejection had cut deeply into her heart and left her bleeding.

"I did not hurt you."

How could he say that? "You pushed me away like I was diseased! You left! You didn't come back. I don't know what you are up to now, but I'm not such a believer in fairy tales that I would entertain for one minute the thought I could be someone special in your life."

A charming smile tilted his lips. "So you see me as Prince Charming and yourself the frog? I assure you, I am more than willing to kiss you and turn you into a princess."

His mockery was the limit. Her eyes burned with tears she did not want to shed in front of him. "Leave me alone, Luciano. Just leave me alone." She spun on her heel and this time she made her escape good. She made it to the bathroom and slammed the door only to discover it had no lock.

She looked around wildly, but there was no escape.

She stared at the knob and willed it to stay immobile accepting she had absolutely no telekinetic powers when the knob turned.

The door opened and Luciano filled the doorway, his dark gaze probing her with tactile intensity. "You have taken me wrong, *bella mia.* It was a little joke. A poor one, but only a joke."

"Get out," she said, her voice breaking on a sob, "I want to freshen up."

He shook his head. "I cannot leave you in such distress."

"Why not? You did six months ago."

"But I did not know so at the time."

"Are you trying to say that if you had, you would have stayed? That you would not have rejected me so publicly and treated me like the kiss meant nothing to you?"

His face was tight with frustration, but he did not answer. Probably because a truthful answer would put him even further in the wrong.

''I didn't think so,'' she said, sounding every bit as cynical as the women who had mocked her at the party.

In a move that shocked her, he reached out and pulled her to him. ''That is in the past. This is now. We begin from here, *cara*.''

She hated her treacherous body that longed to melt against him. ''I'm not up to your speed.'' Miserably aware that it was too true, she tried to pull away. ''I belong with someone like David.''

She stared in mesmerized fascination as his rage went nuclear. ''You belong with me,'' he said with lethal intensity. Then his mouth crashed down on hers.

She thought the New Year's Eve kiss had been hot, but it was nothing like this. Nothing.

Luciano was branding her with his mouth. There was no other way to describe how his lips molded her own, the way his tongue forced entry into her too willing mouth. He tasted the same and yet different. No champagne to dilute the impact of the flavor that was uniquely him.

Hard masculine hands clamped to her waist and lifted. She landed plastered from lips to toe-tips against the ungiving contours of an aroused male body. He aligned her with him so that the evidence of his arousal was pressed into the apex of her thighs. Sliding one hand to her bottom, he manipulated her so that his hardness teased the sensitive flesh of her femininity right through the layers of her clothes.

She'd never known anything so intimate in her life.

She tried to put some distance between them, but she had no leverage with her feet completely off the floor. His hold was too firm to wiggle out of his arms and her efforts in that direction only increased the strange sensations arcing through her from the friction at the juncture of her thighs.

He wrapped his arm around the small of her back and pressed her firmly against him while increasing the intimacy of their kiss. And she melted. Just like she'd done before. Unlike before, however, there was no voice to interrupt and Luciano did not pull away. The urgency in his kiss grew along with the rising passion in her.

She became aware of his hand on her thigh, *under her dress*. How had it gotten there? She should protest, but that would mean breaking the kiss. Besides, his hand on her bare skin felt good. Too good to fight. Knowing fingers burned a trail of erotic caresses up the unprotected skin of her leg until they reached her bottom. He cupped her there and his mouth swallowed the sound of her shock.

Feelings so intense they frightened her coursed through her every nerve ending.

She ached to touch him. She ached for more of his touch. She lost all sense of self-preservation in the face of such overwhelming pleasure and ran her hands over his face, his shoulders, his neck, everywhere she could reach from her position locked against him.

He groaned and moved.

She realized he'd backed up to lean against the vanity when one of her feet bumped the cabinet. He pressed her legs apart and over his thighs, pushing the hard ridge of his arousal into impossibly intimate contact with her body. She didn't have time to contemplate this because suddenly his hand was inside the silk of her panties, touching the naked flesh of her bottom. Goose bumps flashed over her flesh, accompanied by involuntary shivers that had nothing to do with being cold.

In fact, she'd never been so hot in all her life.

That devastating hand went lower to the underside of her bottom. Sliding centimeters to the left, fingers stealthily found her most intimate flesh from an unexpected direction and this time even his mouth covering hers could not stifle the shriek of shock at contact.

The feel of a man's finger pressing into flesh that had never known anyone's touch before was so alien that it shocked her out of the sensual reverie she'd sunk into with his kiss. She squirmed, trying to get away from that intimate touch, but that caused an amazing friction between Luciano's excited male flesh and her sweetest spot.

His big body shuddered.

She tore her mouth from his. "*Luciano*. Please!"

He said something in Italian and started kissing her neck, using his tongue and teeth in a form of erotic teasing that made her squirm even more, but with pleasure this time, not shock.

His head lifted and dark eyes burned her with their sensual force. "You belong to me, *bella mia*. Admit it."

She couldn't deny a truth she'd known somewhere in her heart since she was eighteen years old. "Yes, Luciano, yes." When had she not?

"*Cara!*" His mouth rocked back over hers in another soul-shaking kiss.

It went on and on and she lost all touch with reality.

She could feel only his body beneath hers. She could taste only his mouth. She could smell only his scent. She could hear nothing but their joined heartbeats and a ringing in her ears.

He groaned, breaking his mouth away from hers. It was the sound of a man facing Purdah when Heaven had been within his grasp.

Her head was too heavy for her neck and it dropped forward into the hollow of his neck.

A moment later a discreet cough sounded from the doorway to the guest room. "*Signor* di Valerio."

"*Sì?*" Luciano's voice sounded strained.

"*É la vostra madre.*"

*It is your mother.* The simple Italian phrase penetrated her brain through the fog of arousal still blunting her thinking process.

He said something that sounded suspiciously like a swearword. "I must take the call, *piccola mia.*"

She made a halfhearted attempt at a nod, still too enervated to speak.

He slowly withdrew his hand from intimate contact with her body as if it pained him to do so. She buried her face against him until he gently set her away from him. She kept her eyes fixed on the floor. How could she have made the same mistake twice? She hadn't just let him kiss her, she'd responded with all the wantonness of a woman who routinely shared her body with men. She didn't even know she was capable of that level of abandon to the physical.

It both scared and shamed her.

"Look at me, Hope."

She shook her head. The memory of the way she had allowed him to touch her and where she had let him touch her was sending arrows of mortification into her conscience with bull's-eye accuracy.

"You have nothing to be guilty over."

That was easy for him to say. He was just fruit tasting. She'd never done any of this before. "You would say that," she accused. "You've probably seduced enough women to populate a small town."

His laughter brought her head snapping up as nothing else could have.

She glared at him. "Don't you laugh at me, Luciano di Valerio."

He put his hands out in a gesture of surrender. "I am not the rogue you think me and I was not trying to seduce you."

"Right." What the heck had he been doing then, practicing his technique?

He brushed her hair behind her ear in a tender gesture that made her treacherous heart melt. "You belong to me as no woman has. Do not regret the passion the good God has given us as a gift."

He didn't mean it the way it sounded. He couldn't. He was implying a special relationship. After New Year's Eve and how easily he had turned away and stayed away, she could not afford to let herself read too much into his words.

"You have to answer the phone. You mustn't keep your mother waiting." Hope wanted time to regroup her defenses.

He looked at her as if contemplating saying something more, but in the end, he said only, "I will be with you as quickly as I can," before turning to leave.

Hope availed herself of the toiletries in the well-stocked guest bathroom and tried to ignore the fact they had probably been put there for the convenience

of his women friends. *Like her.* How much importance could she put on his avowal she was different?
Her supposed difference could stem entirely from the
fact that she was a virgin, undoubtedly a rare experience in the life of a male who dated such sophisticated women.

Luciano stopped a few feet from where Hope sat surrounded by the lush greenery and night-blooming
flowers in his terrace garden. Strings of small white
lights illuminated the dining area giving Hope, with
her burnished curls and elfin features, the appearance
of a fairy in her element.

Something untamed twisted inside him at the
thought she could disappear from his life like the fey
wood creature she resembled, leaving nothing behind
but his unsatisfied and unabated arousal. If he had
been shocked by the deliciousness of her response on
New Year's Eve, he was poleaxed by the living flame
he'd held in his arms tonight.

*He wanted her.*

She wanted him too, but she didn't trust him.

Anger surfaced to mix with the desire simmering
inside him as he considered her reasons for feeling
the way she did. She'd been savaged by her grandfather's guests after Luciano had left the party. His
clumsy response to the unexpected carnality of their
kiss had been read as a repudiation of her advances,
when she had made no advances at all.

How had that blonde thought she would get away
with spreading such lies? Had she thought they would
never reach his ears, or that he would not care? She
would learn to regret the mistaken assumption.
Luciano di Valerio did not tolerate being the subject

of a tissue of lies. More importantly, Hope was his now and he protected his own.

His hands curled at his sides and atavistic anticipation curled through him at the thought of dealing with the two men who had propositioned her. They would repent treating an innocent, shy creature with such a lack of respect.

There was a certain amount of gratification in knowing that the marriage would redress the wrong he had done her. His pride still balked at submitting to her grandfather's blackmail, but Luciano could not deny he owed Hope for the humiliation she had suffered at his unwitting hands. Their marriage would even the scales, a very important issue for this Sicilian man.

*Sì*, and there was again no denying that their marriage bed would be a satisfying one. Even now, he wanted to go over there and lift her from the chair, carry her to his bed and finish what they had begun earlier.

Hope felt a prickling sensation on the back of her neck and turned in her chair. Luciano stood a few feet away, a look in his eyes that made the fine hairs on her body stand up. In an instant of primal awareness she could not anticipate or block, all the composure and self-control she had managed to gather around herself in his absence dissipated with the ease of water on an Arizona highway.

"I am sorry to have left you so long." He came toward her, the muscles in his thighs flexing under the perfectly tailored Italian suit he was wearing.

Did the guy ever wear jeans? Probably not and

most likely her heart couldn't stand the sight of him in the tight-fitting denim anyway.

"Don't worry about it. I've been enjoying the view. It's incredible up here."

Luciano's terrace covered the entire portion of the top story of the Valerio building not occupied by his or the company apartments. Someone had turned it into a garden, giving the impression of being in an enchanted bower high above the streets of Athens. The view over the wall was spectacular. The moment she'd seen it she'd been glad she came with Luciano, if only for the opportunity to spend her final evening in Greece in such magical surroundings.

He sat down in the chair opposite hers. No sooner than he had done and a drink was placed in front of him by a discreet servant. The first course was served moments later. They were eating their main course, a meatless moussaka when she realized the entire meal had been vegetarian.

"You remembered I don't care to eat meat." It shocked her. She'd lived with her grandfather since she was five years old and he still couldn't remember that about her. And if he had remembered, he would never have catered to her desires.

"It is not such a big thing." His shoulders moved in a typical throw away gesture. "But tell me, does it bother you to be at the table when others eat it?"

"No, but I don't look too closely at their plates either," she admitted ruefully.

He seemed pleased by that, though she could not imagine what it had to do with him. Their conversation flowed, Luciano asking her questions about her life in Boston and answering her questions about his life in Sicily.

"So, what are you doing in Athens, or is it top-secret business stuff?" She was used to her grandfather keeping tight lips about many areas of his life.

"I make frequent trips to my headquarters here and elsewhere."

He was as driven as her grandfather. "Do you ever take time off to relax?"

His smile sent sensations quivering through her. "I am relaxing now, with you."

"But even this," she indicated their almost finished dinners, "is prompted by your business interests."

"I assure you, business has not been in the forefront of my mind since I spied you walking back toward your tour bus laughing with your companion, your hand in his." His voice had taken on the hardness of tempered steel.

She didn't want a reenactment of their earlier argument, so she opted not to reply to his comment. She chose instead, to change the subject. "How is your mother? Your sister is twenty now, isn't she? Is she dating anyone special?"

For a moment he actually looked bemused. "You know a great deal about me."

"It is inevitable after a five-year acquaintance-ship." Or rather five years of infatuation, she thought with some sadness.

"My mother is fine." He laid his fork down and leaned back against his chair. "She is pressing me to marry soon."

An irrational sense of loss suffused her at his words—irrational because you could not lose what you had never had. He would oblige his mother, she was sure. At thirty, Luciano was of an age for a Sicilian male to start making babies. The thought of another woman big with his child was enough to destroy what remained of her appetite.

"And your sister?" she asked, pushing away her half-finished plate, trying not to dwell on the prospect of him marrying soon.

Warm indulgence lit his almost black eyes. "Martina is enjoying university too much to allow any one male to seriously engage her interest."

"You allowed her to attend university in America, didn't you?" She could remember discussing the merits of different colleges with him a couple of years previously at one of her grandfather's business dinners.

"*Sì*. She enjoys it very much. Mamma worries she will not wish to return to a traditional life in Sicily though."

Hope had nothing to say in reply to that. She had no experience of daughters and mothers. Hers had died when she was much too young.

"It is understandable," Luciano brooded. "Life in Sicily is still very traditional in some ways. Mamma has never worn a pair of trousers in her whole life. If you were seen holding hands with your young blond friend in the small village in the country outside Palermo where I grew up, an engagement announcement might be expected."

Why did he keep harping on that? It had been totally innocent, unlike the kiss they had shared not too long ago. "David is from Texas," she tried to explain. "He's very affectionate, but he doesn't mean anything by it."

His brows rose in mockery. "This is why he invited you back to his room."

Oh, dear. Luciano was back to looking dangerous.

"He's never done that before. He was just reacting to your arrogant claim on me. It's a guy thing, I guess."

"Are you truly so naive you do not realize this man wants you?"

"I'm not naive." Introverted did not equal stupid.

His dark eyes narrowed. "Your inexperience of men and their ways shows in your foolish belief that the touches of a man who pays you particular attention mean nothing."

He didn't need to rub in how gauche she must appear in comparison to his usual date. So, she seemed a fool to him. She must be to have allowed herself to enjoy his kisses and conversation when he thought so little of her. "If you're finished insulting me, I'd like to go back to my hotel now."

"We have not yet had dessert."

"I'm not hungry." She indicated her unfinished dinner. "And we have an early start tomorrow."

"Is it that, or is that you wish to return and keep your liaison with David?" Unbelievably, Luciano sounded jealous.

"I've already told you, I have no intention of sharing David's room tonight." She spoke slowly and through gritted teeth. "But if I did, it wouldn't be any of your business," she added for good measure.

"You can say this after the way you allowed me to touch you not an hour ago?" Outrage vibrated off of him.

Wasn't that just like an arrogant guy used to getting his own way? He'd done the kissing and now held her accountable for it. "I didn't *let* you touch me. You just did it."

"You did not protest." He was six feet, four inches

of offended masculine pride. "You were with me all the way."

Heat scorched into her cheeks at the reminder. "A gentleman would not rub my face in it."

"A *lady* would not go from one man's arms to the bed of another."

She jumped up from her chair, so furious, she could barely speak. "Are you saying I'm some sort of tramp because I let you kiss me?"

He rose to tower over her. "I am saying I will not tolerate you returning to this David's company now that you belong to me."

"I don't belong to you!"

"You do and you will stay here with me."

# CHAPTER FIVE

SHE couldn't believe what she was hearing.

She knew about the possessive streak in the Italian temperament, but to say she belonged to him just because they'd kissed was ludicrous. Not only was it ridiculous, it was inconsistent as anything. He certainly hadn't been singing that tune New Year's Eve.

"Then why didn't I belong to you six months ago? Why did you leave and not come back? *I'll tell you why,*" she went on before he had a chance to answer, *"because those kisses meant no more to you than eating a chocolate bar.* You found them pleasant, but not enough to buy the candy store."

"You expected marriage after one kiss?" His derision hit her on the raw.

"You're deliberately misunderstanding me. I didn't say anything of the kind. You're the one who has been rabbiting on about me belonging to you because of an inconsequential kiss."

"Hardly inconsequential. I could have had you and you would not have murmured so much as a protest."

*Oh.* She wanted to scream. "No doubt your skills in the area of seduction are stellar, but what does that signify? With my limited experience in the area, any man with a halfway decent knowledge of a woman's reactions could have affected me just as strongly."

She didn't believe it for a minute, but Luciano's conceit was staggering. His assertion she would not have protested him taking her to bed might be true, but it was also demeaning.

"You think this?" he demanded, his eyes terrifying in their feral intensity. "Perhaps you intend to experiment with this friend of yours, this David?"

A tactical retreat was called for. "No. I don't want to experiment with anybody, including you."

He didn't look even remotely appeased by her denial.

Good judgment required she not dwell on this particular argument. "I am merely trying to point out that kissing me didn't give you any rights over me. If all the women you kissed belonged to you, you'd have a bigger harem than any Arabian prince in history."

Instead of looking insulted by her indictment of his character, he appeared pleased by her assessment of his masculinity. The fury in his expression faded. "You are different than the other women I have known."

"Known being a discreet euphemism, I assume?" She thought of all the beautiful women he had been photographed with for scandal rags and society pages. It left a hollow place where her heart should have been beating and it made her doubly determined to deny him any claim to her loyalty. "Only you haven't *known* me and I don't belong to you."

"This crudeness is not becoming."

She couldn't deny it. Crude was not her style and she'd probably blush with embarrassment later, but right now she was fighting the effect he had on her with every weapon at her disposal. "Neither is a dog-in-the-manger possessiveness."

"What is this canine in a stable?"

She stared at him. *Canine in a stable?* Suddenly the humor of the situation overcame her. She started to laugh. Here she was arguing with Mr. Cool himself that he didn't have any hold on her when she wanted more than anything for him to claim her as his own. She was nuts, but then so was he. *And* his perfect English had a few flaws.

"You find me amusing?" He didn't look happy about the possibility.

She grabbed at her self-control and reined in her laughter, humor that had taken on a slightly hysterical twinge. "It's not you. It's this situation. Don't you think it's funny that you're standing here asserting rights over me you can't possibly want?"

"If I assert them, I want them," was his arrogant rejoinder.

All the humor fled, hysterical or otherwise, and she swallowed the words that would beg him to repeat what he'd just said. He simply could not mean it the way she wanted him to.

"This isn't about me. This is about David and your reaction to him. You acted like two dogs fighting over a bone back at the Parthenon. Now, *you* are trying to bury the bone, not because you really want it, but because you don't want him to have it. Well, I'm not going to stay buried just to please your sense of male superiority."

She'd spent most of her life in the background and she was tired of it. Why the realization should come now, she didn't know and she didn't care. Luciano didn't really want her. He wanted to one-up David. She wasn't entirely sure about David's motives, but that wasn't the issue. The issue was *her life and what she was going to do with it.*

The simple answer was live it.

On her terms.

Starting now.

"I'm going back to my hotel. You can have your chauffeur drive me or I can catch a cab, but I'm ready to leave."

Her determination must have gotten through to him because his jaw tightened, but he nodded. "I will return you to your hotel."

"There is no need for you to accompany me."

"There is every need," he growled.

Since she was getting her way about leaving, she decided not to argue about this. If he wanted to waste his time riding in the limo with her to see her to her hotel, then let him. She was also through trying to protect everyone but herself from being put upon.

The ride back to her hotel happened in silence. Luciano was too angry to talk without giving away the state of his emotions and no way was he going to allow her to know the extent of her effect on him. Shy she might be. Innocent sexually, even. But still she was a woman and emotions were the weapons of choice for the female of the species.

He could not believe the turn the evening had taken. He had thought after their kiss, she would recognize his claim on her. Her assertion that she did not belong to him had both shocked and enraged him. His quiet little kitten had claws and an independence he would not have suspected.

He needed to rethink his campaign. The time limit her grandfather had set was fast approaching. He had to get her agreement soon in order to have sufficient weeks to plan a Sicilian wedding. Anything less would hurt Mamma.

Hope reached out to open the door the minute the car stopped. Luciano allowed her to exit the car without protest, but he followed her.

She turned, her pansy eyes widening when she realized he was right behind her rather than seated safely in the car. She would not get rid of him so easily.

She put her hand out. "Thank you for an interesting evening. The food was wonderful and you could charge admission on the view from your terrace."

She said nothing about the company and he felt the urge to smile at her spirit in spite of his anger.

He took her hand, but instead of shaking it, used it to pull her into his body, so he could walk her inside. "I will take you to your room."

Her small body was stiff in his hold. "I won't argue because it won't do me any good to tell you I would rather walk alone."

His lips twisted wryly. "You have said it."

"And it didn't do me any good."

"I would be a poor escort if I did not see you to your door."

"Cro-Magnon man has nothing on you for primitive."

"Good manners are the mark of civilization, not the lack of it."

Her response to that was a disdainful sound that could only be described as a snort.

He led her into the elevator, not displeased by the lack of other guests in the small space. He had indicated to his security team that they should wait outside, so no one was with them to witness her obvious irritation. She was staying on the fourth floor and the ride up in the elevator was charged with silence.

As the doors slid open, he asked, "Which room?"

"Four-twenty-two." She pointed the way with a flick of her hand.

As they walked to her door, he noticed another one further along the hall opening. Blond hair above glowering masculine features identified the spying neighbor as David, the man from Texas. Hope might not accept Luciano's possession, but he was determined that David would recognize the fact of it.

He pulled her to a stop just inside the door and turned her to face him.

"Good night," she said in an obvious attempt at dismissal.

*"Buona notte,"* he replied as his head lowered toward hers.

He watched as her eyes widened and her mouth opened to protest, but his lips prevented the words from expelling. Taking advantage of her open mouth, he slid his tongue inside to taste the sweetness he had quickly learned to crave.

She blinked, her violet eyes darkening even as she tried to push away from him. He moved his hands down her back, pressing one against her ribs and using the other to cup her behind. Her eyes went unfocused and then slid shut as she surrendered to his touch. He kissed her with the intent of claiming her body even if her mind denied the truth of his possession.

He kissed her until he heard a distinct American curse and a slamming door. He kissed her until her body was totally pliant against him and her mouth moved in innocent arousal against his own.

He was tempted to push her back two feet, shut the door and make love to her until she agreed to marry him. He sensed, though, that she would be ashamed afterward, that it would hurt her to be won by such means.

He did not want to hurt her. She was not part of her grandfather's scheme. He was sure of it now.

He would treat her with the respect the future mother of his children deserved.

It was harder than anything he had done since burying his father, but he gently disengaged their bodies and set her away from him.

Her eyes opened. "What…"

He smiled and touched her lips with his forefinger. "You belong to me. Your body knows it and soon your mind will accept it as well."

"What about my heart?" she whispered, her expression dazed.

"It is only right for a woman to love her husband."

Her mouth dropped open. *"Husband?"*

Now would be a good time for a strategic withdrawal. *"Sì.* Husband. Think about it, *tesoro."*

He waited to hear the bolt slide home before he left.

As he walked by the door that had opened earlier, he thought a few words with the young Romeo would not go amiss.

*Think about it.*

Hope shoved her suitcase closed and zipped it shut with undue force.

The fiend.

That was all she'd been doing since last night.

He'd kissed her until her hard-won composure had

melted in the heat of their mutual desire. Then he'd pushed her away and left, but not before making the disturbing announcement he intended to marry her. Well, he hadn't actually said *that*. He'd said a wife should love her husband, but they'd been talking about him and her, so didn't it follow he meant he was thinking of her as his wife?

Only what if he hadn't? What if she was reading all sorts of things into a comment he'd meant in jest. He'd admitted on New Year's Eve that his jokes didn't always come off right.

*But she could have sworn he wasn't joking.* What if he *had* meant it? Luciano di Valerio her husband. The mind boggled. Could she survive marriage to such a devastating man? She'd decided to stop living in the shadows, but she hadn't considered a move so close to the burning power of the sun.

What was that saying about being careful what you wished for? She'd been dreaming of Luciano for the past five years, but she had never considered those dreams could become a reality. They had been safe, a way for her to allay her loneliness. Luciano in the flesh was not safe, as he'd proven each time he had kissed her.

She lost her soul when they kissed. Or found it. Either way, they terrified her—these feelings he could evoke.

And for all his tolerance toward his sister's desire to go to university in America, he was still a traditional Sicilian male in many ways. Look how he had reacted to David holding her hand. While she was a modern, if slightly introverted, American woman. How could a marriage between them work?

She was too independent to accept the long-established role of the Sicilian wife. He was too bossy not to interfere in her life in ways that would no doubt infuriate her.

It was crazy.

She pulled her suitcase off the bed and left it outside the room for the porter to pick up and add to the tour's luggage on the bus.

Contemplating marriage with Luciano was an exercise in futility. He was probably already regretting the kisses they'd shared and the implications he had made.

She walked into the hotel dining room and seeing David at a table by the window, she went toward him. They'd been sharing breakfast since the second day of the tour, sometimes *à deux* and other times joined by their fellow tour members. This morning, he was sitting alone at a table for four.

She slid into the seat opposite him. "Good morning."

He looked up from the paper he'd been reading, *The Dallas Morning News*. He had it special delivered because he said he couldn't stand too many days without news from back home.

His usually mobile face remained impassive. "Is it?"

He was still angry about her choosing to go with Luciano instead of him the night before. "Did you end up going back to the Psiri?" she asked with a tentative smile.

"What's it to you if I did?"

She started at the belligerence in his voice. "I think I'll order my breakfast." She signaled for the waiter.

"Are you sure you want to do that?"

"Why wouldn't I?" What was the matter with him this morning?

"Your boyfriend might take offense to you eating breakfast with me."

"I don't have a boyfriend."

"That's not the way it looked last night."

She sighed. "I'm sorry if you were disappointed I didn't have dinner with you last night, but you shouldn't have taken for granted that you could schedule my time."

"I realize that now."

Good. At least that had worked out from last night's fiasco. She smiled. "No harm done."

"Not for you. It must be nice having two men fighting for your attention, but personally I think your ploy was juvenile."

"What ploy?" she demanded, getting irritated by his continued innuendo that she did not understand.

"You should have told me you belonged to someone else. You let me think you were unattached."

"I am unattached." Did all men think in terms of belonging? Perhaps only the strong, arrogant ones. "Furthermore, this is the twenty-first century for heaven's sake. I belong to myself, thank you very much."

David snorted at that. "Not according to your Italian boyfriend."

*"He's not my boyfriend,"* she gritted out between clenched teeth.

"Right. That's why you went with him last night instead of having dinner with me."

She wasn't going to admit she'd been virtually kidnapped after making her grand declaration about eating alone. It made her seem feeble and she wasn't, but she had been outflanked.

"Are you saying that my having dinner with a man automatically makes him my boyfriend?" He was more medieval than Luciano.

"It was a hell of lot more than dinner from where I stood."

"What are you talking about?"

"I was in my room when you returned to the hotel last night."

"So?"

"I saw him kiss you. Afterward he paid me a visit and told me in very clear terms just whose woman you are." Anger and wounded pride vibrated in David's voice.

"He had no right to do that." More importantly though was why had he? She could not wrap her mind around the concept of Luciano being so possessive of her.

David's blue eyes narrowed. "He had his hand on your butt and his tongue down your throat. If he's not your boyfriend, what does that make you?"

The offensive description of Luciano's passionate good-night kiss shocked her. Up until the night before, David had been an affable and rather mild companion.

"What exactly are you implying?"

David tossed the paper on the table and stood up. "You let him paw you in a public hallway and you've never even given me the green light to kiss you goodnight. You figure it out."

She watched David walk away feeling both grief and anger. It hurt that David was willing to dismiss their friendship so easily, but his implication that she lacked morals really rankled. She was an anachronistic virgin in a world of sexual gluttony, for goodness' sake. She did not sleep around.

Had Luciano been right in his assessment of David's motives? David had not reacted as a simple friend to the events of last night. Had he been angling to share her bed?

It wouldn't be the first such relationship to develop in their tour group, but she would have considered herself the least likely candidate for one. She didn't have any experience with men wanting her.

David certainly seemed offended this morning that she'd allowed Luciano to kiss her last night, but she still could not quite believe it was about David wanting her. More likely it was that dog fighting over a bone thing again.

However Luciano's actions weren't as easy to explain, at least not in a way that didn't seem too farfetched. Luciano di Valerio wanting to marry Hope Bishop? Not likely. Yet, that is what he had implied. Then he had gone out of his way to warn David off.

Put together, those two items were enough to prevent relaxed slumber over the next four nights.

Hope woke up feeling cranky and out of sorts the day they were scheduled to tour Pompeii. This was their fifth day in Italy and Luciano had not made another appearance. He'd managed to find her in Greece, but now that they were in his home country...nothing. And Naples was not exactly the other side of the world from Palermo. The man was a billionaire. He had a helicopter, not to mention a jet.

If it were important for him to see her, as he'd implied, wouldn't he have used one of them?

David had gotten over his snit by the time they arrived in Rome and apologized sweetly for his accusations. They'd agreed to resume their friendship and had toured the Vatican together. Their relationship wasn't as free and easy as it had been. She was careful to avoid his casual touches, afraid Luciano had been right. In allowing it, perhaps she had encouraged David to think she wanted something from their friendship that she didn't.

She yawned behind her hand as she entered the hotel dining room. If she didn't start getting some sleep soon, she was in trouble, but her dreams were filled with a tall Sicilian man and her waking thoughts were tormented by his comment about marriage.

"You are tired, *tesoro*. This tour is perhaps not such a good thing for you."

Her head whipped around and there he stood.

"Luciano, what are you doing here?" As greetings went, it was not original. She excused herself with her fatigue and shock at seeing him right when she was thinking of him.

"Surely you are not surprised to see me."

"But I am. It's been almost a week."

His brow rose in mockery. "And you expected me to show up before this?"

"No. Well…" She didn't want to lie, but she wasn't handing it to him in his lap either.

"I was called to New York on a business emergency."

"You could have called. Grandfather has my cell phone number." He was the one, after all, who had said she was different.

"I did not think of this." He looked chagrined by the admission.

She felt a smile spreading over her face. "That's all right then, but why have you come today?"

"I desire to escort you around Pompeii."

"I'd like that." Nearly five days had been enough time for her to realize that if Luciano wanted to pursue a relationship with her, she would be the world's biggest fool to deny him.

A love that had not abated in five years was not going to go away. If she wanted a chance at a husband and a family, she accepted it would be with him, or not at all. If nothing else, her renewed friendship with David had taught her that. She had no desire to pursue anything personal with him and had not been the least bit jealous when another woman on the tour had begun flirting with him.

They were together now, at a table for two.

Luciano proved his gaze had followed hers when he said, "So, he accepted he could not have you and has transferred his interests."

"You shouldn't have gone to his room that night," she chided.

"You did not yet recognize you were mine, but I made certain he did. It was necessary to avoid complications."

She sighed. It was no use arguing with him about it. What was done was done and she couldn't say she was sorry.

"No comeback?" Dark brown eyes pinned her own gaze with probing concentration.

She shook her head.

"You are mine?"

"Are you asking me?" That was new.

"I am asking if you accept it."

If she denied it, she would be lying to both of them.

He hadn't meant to hurt her with his rejection on New Year's Eve and she had to trust him not to hurt her now. She had no choice. She wanted him beyond pride or reason, so she took the plunge. "Yes."

# CHAPTER SIX

Luciano dismissed the emotion he experienced at her acknowledgment as natural relief that his plan was back on course. The sooner Hope became his, the closer he would be to regaining control of Valerio Shipping.

"At last, we progress."

She grimaced at his choice of words, but did not demur.

Smiling, he took her arm and led her to a table. Her acquiescence now was in marked contrast to her vehement protest a week ago when he had been forced to practically kidnap her in order to secure her company for the evening. He helped her into her seat brushing a light kiss against her temple as he did so. Startled pansy eyes took him in as he crossed to sit on the other side of the intimate table for two.

Even after the intimacies they had shared, she still acted surprised when he touched her.

He liked the shyness.

He had already ordered breakfast for them, but he waved the waiter over to fill her coffee cup. "You do look tired, *piccola mia.*" Her eyes were bruised and her complexion pale from an obvious lack of sleep. "Perhaps we should put the tour of Pompeii off for another day."

She hid a yawn behind one small hand. "I can't. Today's our last day in Naples. Tomorrow we fly to Barcelona."

"I do not wish for you to leave Italy."

Her violet eyes widened, but she did not fly at him in anger as she had done before when he told her he wanted her to leave the tour. "I have two weeks left of my European visit."

"Spend them in Palermo with my family. Mamma wishes to meet you and Martina is home from university. She will enjoy the companionship of someone closer to her own age."

"You told your mother about me?"

"*Sì.*" She would have been very hurt if he had sprung a bride on her out of the blue. She was not overly pleased that Hope was American rather than Sicilian, but the prospect of grandchildren outweighed even that drawback.

"What did you tell her?" Hope was looking at him as if he'd grown donkey ears.

"Why the shock?" He had told Hope his intentions. "I told Mamma I had met a woman I wanted for *mi moglie,* my wife."

"I know what the word means." She took a gulp of coffee and then started coughing.

He was around the table in a moment, pressing a glass of water into her hands. "Are you all right?"

"Yes. It was too hot."

"Be more careful, *carina.* If you burn your mouth, how can I kiss it?"

She blushed and set the glass of water down with a trembling hand as he resumed his seat.

"I wasn't sure you were serious, about marriage I mean." Again the charming blush.

"I am."

She nodded, the soft chestnut curls around her face bouncing. "I can see that, but it's such a shock."

To him as well. He had not been anticipating marriage just yet, particularly to a shy American virgin. "Life is not so easily predicted."

"I suppose you're right."

"So, will you come to Sicily with me and stay in my home with my mother and sister?"

"I don't know."

He stifled his impatience. She was skittish, like an untried mare. He did not want to spook her when his plans were finally working out as he had originally expected. Perhaps the emergency in New York had been a gift from the good God because it had given her time to make up her mind to him.

"What makes you hesitate?" he asked, allowing none of his impatience to show in his voice. "Are you concerned for your virtue? Mamma will act as sufficient chaperone surely."

"I'm not worried about that. I'm twenty-three years old. I don't need your mother's protection."

He smiled at her feistiness. "What then?"

"Grandfather might not like it."

"I have already spoken to your grandfather."

"You have?" Once again she looked like a doe startled by an unexpected sound.

"*Sì.* It is only natural I should speak to him when I wish to marry his granddaughter." He said nothing of the fact Reynolds had been the one to instigate the meeting. That was not relevant to Luciano and Hope. He wanted to marry her. That was the only issue she need be concerned with.

"How can you say that so calmly?"

"Say what?" he asked.

"That bit about wanting to marry me. I mean we haven't even led up to it and suddenly, boom, here you are saying you want to marry me like it's a fore-gone conclusion. You haven't even asked me.''

Nor had he courted her and a woman deserved to be courted to marriage. But... ''Have we not led up to it? The kiss we shared on New Year's Eve, the kisses we shared last week, they lead to bed and bed with a virgin means marriage for this Italian male.''

Her pale skin took on a fiercely rosy hue. ''That's not what I meant.''

''Do you still deny the way we kissed gave me claim to you?'' He had thought they were past that.

''No, but marriage is not necessarily the next in-evitable step.''

''It is.''

''Come on, Luciano. Like I've said before, you can't tell me you marry every woman you kiss pas-sionately.''

Had he ever shared a passion so volatile with an-other woman? He did not think so. ''I have never kissed another virgin.''

''Hush!'' She looked around, her expression almost comical. ''This is not the place to discuss my sexual experience, or lack thereof.''

''I agree.'' It was exciting him to think of intro-ducing her into the pleasures of the flesh. He wanted to be able to walk when they left the restaurant, but if they didn't change the subject he wasn't going to be able to.

''Come to Palermo and let me convince you.''

''You mean like a courtship?''

''Sì. Exactly.''

''I didn't think men still did that.''

''It is a ritual that will continue through the mil-lennia, whatever you choose to call it. Men will pursue their chosen mate with whatever means at their disposal.''

''And your means are a couple of weeks in Palermo with your family?'' She sounded bemused, shocked even.

''*Sì.*''

''All right.''

Hope stretched lazily beside the pool. Rhythmic splashing told her without having to look that Luciano's sister was still swimming laps. Martina was a sweet girl. Three years Hope's junior, she was very Sicilian in some things, but the influence of her years at American university was unmistakable.

She didn't defer to her brother as if he were a deity and she had no desire to marry a man solely to secure her future.

Smart and independent, Martina had made life in the di Valerio household bearable for Hope. Not that Luciano's mother was unbearable. Quite the opposite. She was kindness itself, but she took the marriage of her son and his American girlfriend as a foregone conclusion. Just yesterday she had completely unnerved Hope by insisting she be measured for a wedding gown.

When Hope had mentioned this to Luciano, he had merely smiled and complimented his mother on her forward thinking. Evidently, neither he nor his mother had any doubt as to the outcome of Hope's time in Palermo. The prospect of a lifetime married to such a confident male was more than daunting, it was scary.

Because Hope wasn't that confident.

She should be. He made his desire to marry her

very clear as well as his pleasure in her company. In short, he was doing exactly as he said he would do and courting her. While he had to work several hours each day, he spent some time each morning and the evenings with her, either taking her out or having his friends in to meet her.

None of them seemed to find it as odd as she did that he'd chosen a little peahen for his proposed bride rather than a bird of more exotic plumage. But then Italian men of Luciano's income bracket didn't always consider their wives to be the one for show-off potential. They left that job to their mistresses. Did Luciano intend to have a mistress? Did he have one now?

It was a question she had to have answered before she could marry him, but she was afraid to ask. She spent an inordinate amount of time convincing herself she didn't need to. Sometimes it worked. Why wouldn't it?

She had a room that resembled a romantic bower because of all the flowers he had given her, but flowers were the least of his offerings to convince her she wanted to marry him. He gave her gifts practically every day. The bikini she was sunbathing in had been yesterday's present.

He was spoiling her rotten with both time and gifts.

But he said nothing of love and had not kissed her again since her arrival in Palermo. He had said her virtue was safe, but she had not thought that meant all physical attention would cease.

He avoided touching her which bothered her because she'd come to see that Luciano was a tactile man. He hugged his sister frequently, kissed his mother's cheeks coming and going and was very

Italian in his dealing with his friends. Only she was left out of the magical circle of his affection.

Should it be that way when a man wanted to marry a woman?

While she grew more aware of his physical perfection each day, she worried he had lost interest in her body. Yet, would a man as virile as Luciano contemplate marriage to a woman he didn't want? The answer had to be no. Unless he planned to have a mistress. But then why get married at all?

Her mind spun in now familiar patterns.

"What are you thinking about so hard that you didn't hear me calling you?" Martina stood above Hope, her Italian beauty vibrant while she toweled the wetness from her long black hair.

Hope sighed. "Guess."

"My brother."

"Got it in one."

"You are going to marry him, aren't you?" Unexpected anxiety laced Martina's voice.

"I don't know."

"How can you not know? The man is besotted. He gave you that totally naff book of Italian poetry."

"I can't read Italian."

"You're learning."

She was. Her very rudimentary knowledge of the language was growing rapidly. And because of that she was absolutely certain Luciano had never said a single word about loving her, or being besotted even, in either Italian or English.

Martina settled on the lounger next to Hope. "You love him."

"I'm not saying anything on the grounds it could incriminate me. It's the Fifth Amendment of the U.S.

Constitution, you know. Even nosy little sisters can't bypass fundamental rights.''

Martina laughed. ''I don't need you to confirm it. Every time you look at him, you about swallow him alive with your eyes. You are too sweet, not to mention deep, to have a simple lust infatuation for my brother. With a woman like you, desire is linked to love or it wouldn't be there.''

And her desire was obvious to even Luciano's sister. No wonder both Luciano and his mother were so sure of her. ''A woman like me?'' What made her so different? ''Are you saying you're capable of wanting a man to make love to you that you don't love?''

She'd never felt free talking about this sort of stuff with her girlfriends at school. She'd always been too shy, but Martina had steamrolled right over her reticence and they had become confidantes.

Martina giggled. ''Maybe not make love, but I have kissed a few.''

Hope's heart twitched. She could not say the same. She'd hardly ever been kissed and never like Luciano kissed her except by him. She'd never wanted it with another man. ''I suppose it must be love.''

''I knew it.'' Martina clapped her hands. ''You are going to marry him. Mamma's sure of it, you know.''

*''I know.''* How could she miss it having been fitted for the wedding gown, for Heaven's sake?

''She's just dying for grandbabies.''

''What if I don't want to get pregnant right away?''

''I don't think Luciano would like that,'' Martina said candidly, concern in her voice.

Hope secretly agreed. She was becoming more and more convinced that the reason he was considering marriage now, with her, was for those *bambini* every Italian male supposedly wanted.

"Well, it's a nonissue at the moment. Your brother hasn't actually asked me to marry him. Until he does, this is all conjecture."

"Because you're not sure he's going to or because you're still trying to convince yourself you don't know if you'll say yes?"

"*Santo cielo!* Had I known the swimsuit was so revealing I would have bought another one."

"*Ciao,* Luciano. I think Hope looks smashing in the bikini, but you're right. It shows a lot more of her than the one-piece she brought with her."

Hope looked up at Luciano and smiled. "You're both being silly. It's very conservative for a bikini."

And it was. The tank style top showed the barest hint of her cleavage and the hip-hugging short bottoms didn't reveal anything like the thongs she'd seen on the local beaches, or even the high-cut brief bottoms. On her smallish figure, it was perfectly decent.

"Not conservative enough," Luciano muttered in a driven undertone.

"If it bothers you so much—" she began to say.

"Don't offer to change it. You must start as you mean to go on," Martina exclaimed. "If you let him dictate your clothes now, it will never end."

Dark flags of color accentuated Luciano's sculpted cheekbones and warning lights blazed in his deep brown eyes.

"I was going to say, no one was forcing him to look, Miss Smarty Pants." She smiled up at Luciano. "You're back earlier than expected."

"*Sì.* We have been invited to a pool party at the

DeBrecos'. My friend is celebrating the close of a business deal that has given him some trouble.''

''Marco is having a pool party?'' Martina's interest was definitely piqued.

''He is.''

''Am I invited?''

''Of course.''

She jumped up from her lounger. ''I'll go get ready. When do we leave?''

''In less than an hour, *sorella picolla*. Do not make us late applying makeup and effecting an elaborate hairstyle your first dive in the pool will wash away.''

Martina turned to Hope and rolled her lovely brown eyes so like her brother's. ''*Men*. Don't *you* go changing your swimsuit to make him happy.''

''How could I? It was a gift and it would undoubtedly offend your brother for me to reject it in favor of my old swimsuit.''

''Do not bet on it,'' Luciano growled.

Hope laughed. Would a man who did not want her be so affected by her conservative suit? She hoped the answer was no, but she was definitely leaving the suit on. If she could tempt him, at least a little, maybe he would reveal some of his feelings regarding her.

That optimistic belief seemed in vain as Luciano treated her to yet another dose of the courteous, non-touching companion of the past few days at the DeBrecos' pool party.

Feeling desperate to provoke some kind of response, she took off her swimsuit cover and dug in her bag for a bottle of high-factor sunscreen. She turned to Luciano. Wearing only black swim shorts, every rippling muscle in his body was on display and it was all she could do not to drool.

Or trip him and beat him to the ground.

She extended the lotion to him. "Would you do my back? I think what I applied earlier is wearing off and I don't want to burn."

Luciano took the bottle, a strange expression on his face. "You cannot reach your own back, *cara?*"

It wasn't her back she found impossible to reach. It was him! She tried for a nonchalant shrug. "It's easier if you do it."

She turned and presented her back to him, pulling her curly hair from the nape of her neck.

Then two things happened.

Martina dropped gracefully on the lounger beside Hope. "Isn't this great?"

And Marco waved from the other side of the pool, catching Luciano's attention.

He dropped the sunscreen in Martina's lap with more speed than finesse. "Put some of this on Hope's back, *sorella picolla,* while I go see what it is that Marco wants."

Hope watched him go with despair. It wasn't working.

Martina looked at Hope. "Didn't you slather yourself in this stuff before we left the house?"

Hope frowned. "Yes."

"Then why does my brother want me to put more on you? Not only are you limber enough to reach your own back, but you bought the lotion that lasts for hours, even in the water."

Hope hated admitting that she'd tried one of the oldest tricks in the book and it had failed, so she shrugged and reached for the bottle. "Let me put that away."

Martina was looking quizzically at her, then her expression cleared. "I get it. You—"

"Never mind, just hand me the bottle," she said shortly, interrupting Martina before she could put voice to Hope's idiocy.

Martina handed her the lotion, her expression curious. "You know. I noticed that Luciano never touches you."

"I am aware of that." Hope sighed and shoved the plastic bottle back in her bag. Short of making a blatant request, she wasn't going to change that state of affairs either. Even then, she had her doubts.

"That's weird for a guy who wants to marry you."

Hope didn't need the reminder. *"I know."* She glowered at Luciano where he stood talking to Marco.

"What's she doing here?" Martina sounded outraged.

Hope turned her head to look where the younger girl's gaze was directed and felt her heart skip not one, but two beats. This was just what she needed. Zia Merone. She and Luciano had been photographed together several times for the society columns and scandal rags the year before. Rumors of a relationship between the two of them had been rife. Which was a lot more understandable than his name being linked with Hope's. Zia was beautiful and blond, even if it came from a bottle. Taller than Hope by at least six inches, she had a body that was centerfold material.

A little too blousy for a *Vogue* cover, but just what a passionate Sicilian male like Luciano would find attractive.

Hope chewed on her lower lip, tasting blood and

her own jealousy. A most unenviable emotion. "I guess Marco invited her."

"You're right of course, but you'd think she would have enough tact not to come." Martina turned to face her, dark brown eyes snapping with indignation. "Everyone knows you're Luciano's new girlfriend."

"Do they? Maybe she's out of the loop." Hope was watching Zia's progress toward their host and Luciano with a sinking feeling in her heart.

Marco greeted Zia with a kiss on each cheek. Luciano started to do the same, but the model turned her head and caught his lips. The kiss didn't last long and Luciano pulled back with a laugh and said something Hope could not hear from her position on the other side of the pool. The greeting was a throwaway gesture, nothing all that intimate for an Italian male, but after being treated like the untouchable woman for days, it was way too much for Hope.

She jumped up. "I'm going into the house. The sun's too bright right now."

Martina followed her. "Don't worry about it, Hope," she said as she rushed after her. "It was just a little kiss. Believe me, if Luciano had wanted her, he would have kept on kissing her." Apparently realizing that that was not the most tactful thing to say, Martina shut up.

Hope ignored her and increased her pace to warp speed. He didn't kiss *her* at all.

One of Martina's friends grabbed the younger girl and dragged her off. Much to Hope's relief. She liked Luciano's little sister, but she was afraid she was about to cry and she didn't want an audience. She was searching for a bathroom when a male voice

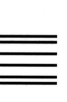

# BUSINESS REPLY MAIL

FIRST-CLASS MAIL    PERMIT NO. 717-003    BUFFALO, NY

POSTAGE WILL BE PAID BY ADDRESSEE

**HARLEQUIN READER SERVICE**
**3010 WALDEN AVE**
**PO BOX 1867**
**BUFFALO NY 14240-9952**

# Get FREE BOOKS and
# FREE GIFTS when you play the...

# LAS VEGAS
## GAME

*Just scratch off
the gold box with a coin.
Then check below to see
the gifts you get!*

## YES! I have scratched off the gold box. Please send me my **2 FREE BOOKS** and **2 FREE GIFTS for which I qualify.** I understand that I am under no obligation to purchase any books as explained on the back of this card.

**306 HDL EF46**        **106 HDL EF56**

FIRST NAME      LAST NAME

ADDRESS

APT.#      CITY

STATE/PROV.      ZIP/POSTAL CODE      (H-P-02/07)

| 7 | 7 | 7 | Worth TWO FREE BOOKS plus TWO BONUS Mystery Gifts! |
| 🍒 | 🍒 | 🍒 | Worth TWO FREE BOOKS! |
| 🔔 | 🔔 | ♣ | TRY AGAIN! |

www.eHarlequin.com

Offer limited to one per household and not
valid to current Harlequin Presents® subscribers. All orders subject to approval.

**Your Privacy -** Harlequin is committed to protecting your privacy. Our privacy policy is available online at www.eHarlequin.com or upon request from the Harlequin Reader Service. From time to time we make our lists of customers available to reputable firms who may have a product or service of interest to you. If you would prefer for us not to share your name and address, please check here. ☐

halted her. He was speaking Italian. She didn't quite catch the rapidly delivered words and turned.

"I'm sorry, I didn't get that," she said in English, hoping he spoke it as well. Then, just in case, she told him in Italian that she didn't speak the language very well.

He smiled. "Ah, you are the American girlfriend."

"Excuse me?" He made it sound like she was an alien being.

"Luciano has brought you home to meet his Mamma."

The man speaking was about her age and beautiful. There was no other way to describe him. Curly brown hair fell in boyish appeal over his forehead, but his body was anything but boyishly proportioned. Perfectly bronzed, he had sculpted muscles and the classic beauty of a Greek statue. He wasn't nearly as tall as Luciano, but he was still taller than Hope and he was smiling at her.

Hope managed a small smile in return. "Martina said everyone knew, but I thought she was exaggerating."

The man shrugged. "Gossip like that spreads fast. I am Giuseppe, Marco's cousin, and you are Hope, Luciano's American girlfriend."

He took her hand and brought it to his lips. The kiss lingered just one second longer than strict courtesy allowed. Letting her hand lower, but not releasing it, he looked her over from head to foot in a manner that made her blush. *"Bellisima!"* And he kissed his fingertips in a gesture of obvious approval.

*Most beautiful.* At least someone thought she was more than a stick of furniture. She smiled again, blushing more intensely with shyness and pleasure. "Thank you."

"Ah this shy little smile, this blush, it is most charming. Combined with your loveliness, it is easy to see what has my friend so enthralled."

"Is he your friend?" she asked, not remembering any mention of a Giuseppe DeBreco. But then she hardly could have met all of Luciano's friends in a few short days.

Giuseppe's lips curved in the smile of an angel. "Of course."

Nevertheless, she tugged at her hand. He let go with a comical look of regret and she found herself grinning at him.

"You are inside the house for a reason?" he asked. "Perhaps you wish to protect such beautiful pale skin from the harsh rays of our Sicilian sun?"

"Something like that." She wasn't about to admit to a perfect stranger that the sight of Luciano with his old girlfriend had sent her running.

"Then come, I will get you a drink and keep you company in the *sala*. You are a guest of my family. You must be entertained."

No longer feeling on the verge of tears, she more than willingly followed the attractive man who wanted *her* company, not that of some other woman. Her conscience tried to tell her that Luciano had been with Marco when Zia had approached him, but she dismissed it. She was in no mood to give him the benefit of the doubt.

Once in the *sala,* Giuseppe went to the minibar against one wall. "I will get you a drink now."

She was expecting something innocuous like lemonade, but he opened a bottle of champagne from the small fridge behind the minibar.

"We'll toast my friend's capture by the beautiful American."

"He's not exactly caught." But she took the glass of champagne he offered and sipped obediently.

Giuseppe mocked her words with his eyes. "You were measured for a wedding gown."

She choked on her champagne. When she could breathe normally, she said, "You're right. Gossip does spread fast."

He shrugged.

"Just for the record," she said, feeling more militant by the mouthful of champagne, "Luciano and I are not engaged."

"Ah, so there is still hope for me," Giuseppe said with exaggerated delight, making her giggle. "Do you wish to listen to music, perhaps watch some television?"

"Maybe some music, but you don't have to stay here and entertain me. I'm very adept at keeping my own company."

He looked scandalized by the very thought. "I am a gentleman. I would never leave a lady to her own devices in the home of my family."

He really was an outrageous flirt. "I don't suppose you play gin rummy?" She had a sudden hankering for the game she played at lunch every day with her friend and co-worker, Edward.

"I am better at poker than gin rummy," Giuseppe said with a wink.

"You know what it is?" she asked in surprise, not responding to his remark about poker.

"Yes. I have an American friend with a passion for

the game. I will locate a deck of cards to amuse you if you like.''

She took another sip of champagne. ''I'd like that. If you play gin rummy with me, I'll play poker with you,'' she promised.

''So, we will both indulge our vices.''

That sounded good to her. She wasn't indulging any vices with Luciano.

Giuseppe was back within a minute, a deck of cards in his hand. While he amused her with stories of Luciano's friends, they played a game of gin rummy. They had only played a couple of hands when it became apparent she would win. On her second glass of champagne, she was feeling warm and benevolent when she went out for the last time.

So, although she would much rather have played another game of rummy, when Giuseppe's frown told her he did not like to lose, she offered to play poker. ''I'm terrible and you're sure to win,'' she said consolingly.

He laughed out loud. ''You know the Sicilian male, he does not like to lose, eh?''

''This is very true. He particularly does not like to lose his woman only to find her entertaining herself with another man.'' The freezing tones of Luciano's voice came from the doorway to the *sala.*

## CHAPTER SEVEN

GIUSEPPE looked up, his expression indolent. "Ah, it is the inattentive boyfriend. A man must accept the risks when he leaves his companion to her own devices, my friend."

Hope said nothing because she agreed. Furthermore, tipsy on champagne, she was in no mood to appease Luciano's stupid male ego when he'd been grinding hers into the dust. Memories of roses and other gifts rose to taunt her conscience and she quickly dispelled them. She didn't want to think about how kind and attentive he'd been when she could still remember the sight of his lips locking with Zia's.

Brief or not, it had been a kiss.

"You have nothing to say?" he demanded of her.

"I was just about to play a game of poker with Giuseppe, but I don't have any money." She indicated her swimsuit-clad body and lack of a bag with a negligent wave of her hand. "Can I borrow some?"

Luciano's expression went flint hard. "No."

She sighed and turned to Giuseppe. "I don't suppose you'd be willing to bet in kind, would you?"

"In kind?" he asked, looking at her as if she was a strangely fascinating creature.

"You know, let me bet something other than money?"

Giuseppe's eyes widened as a strangled sound reached her from the doorway.

She ignored it. "It can't be my clothes though. I'm too shy to play strip poker and besides you'd have the advantage." In actual fact, she was thinking more along the lines of an IOU, but why be boring and say so?

Giuseppe looked at her glass of champagne, which was almost empty and back at her. "You don't drink much, do you?"

"What? No. I don't. Has that got something to do with playing poker? I'm sure I'm not too tipsy to read the cards, if that's what's worrying you."

His gaze slid sideways to a glowering Luciano and back to her. "Not precisely, no."

"You are not playing poker."

She didn't bother to acknowledge Luciano. She smiled at Giuseppe. "So, what can I bet?"

"Luciano does not want you to play." He spoke slowly, as if she might not have gotten the message the first time around when Luciano had said it in such a bossy tone.

"I'm an American woman, you know. We're not that great at being told what to do. For that matter, I'm not sure many modern women are."

"Even the shy ones, I see." His brown eyes twinkled with a level of amusement unwarranted by the situation.

"Giuseppe," Luciano interrupted in a voice that could have razed steel, "I believe Marco would like your help entertaining his guests."

"I am sorry, Hope. I must go." The younger man stood, his angelic smile marked with overtones of real humor. "Duty calls. Perhaps we will get our game of poker another time."

She sighed. "All right. I promise to let you win."

He inclined his head toward her. "I will look forward to it." Then he left.

She picked up the deck of cards, shuffled them, and then laid out the pattern for a game of solitaire. She'd been deprived of her gin rummy partner, but that didn't mean she had to return to poolside to watch Zia fawning over Luciano.

She'd moved three times when she felt his brooding presence right behind her. "Why were you in here playing cards with Giuseppe?"

She didn't bother to turn to face him, but shrugged. "I wanted to."

"I do not like finding you alone with other men." He sounded like a guy trying really hard to hold on to his patience.

"Really?" Well, she didn't like him letting other women kiss him, so they were even. "I'll remember that."

"And not do it again?" His voice was dangerously soft, but the champagne had affected more than her willingness to let Giuseppe win at cards.

"I didn't say that. I enjoyed playing gin rummy with Giuseppe. He's a very nice man. He's really good looking too," she said with more candor than wisdom, "and not so tall that he's overwhelming to a shrimp like me."

Really, she should go for a guy like that instead of the ultra-masculine Luciano. Why weren't hearts more logical?

A sharply indrawn breath behind her told her that he had not liked the provoking answer. "You prefer his company to mine?" His voice was quiet and yet she just knew he was majorly furious at the idea.

An honest answer would be too good for his ego.

"I don't know," she surprised herself by saying. Apparently she wasn't done being provoking. Maybe she should drink champagne more often. She studied her cards. "I only got to play one game of gin rummy with him before you came in and chased him off."

Masculine rage radiated from Luciano in palpable waves that burned against her back. "Yet, you think you might, given the opportunity?"

She moved a red five onto a black six. "He touched me. You don't. Maybe." Liar. She wanted only Luciano.

"He touched you?" The deadly softness of his voice warned her that she had phrased that very badly.

She spun in her chair to face him and regretted the action at once. First and foremost because it made her dizzy, but secondly because his expression was frightening. He looked like he wanted to kill someone and she thought that person might be Giuseppe. She didn't want to cause any problems between the two men, especially when the younger one had been so nice to her.

She glared at Luciano. "Not like that. I'm not like your other girlfriend, Zia. I don't go kissing men in public places."

Luciano ignored the reference to Zia. "How did he touch you, *tesoro?* Tell me." His voice was deadly soft.

"He kissed my hand and he called me beautiful. If you want the truth, it made me feel nice." A lot nicer than having Luciano dump the suntan lotion in his sister's lap and leave with the speed of an Olympic athlete when Marco signaled for him. "Now go back to your *Playboy* Bunny and let me finish my game of solitaire in peace."

Had she really said that? She sounded like a tru-culent child, or a jealous woman. Which she was, she admitted.

"I have no interest in other women and I do not wish to leave you alone."

She rolled her eyes. Right. "Why not?" He had a very strange way of showing his supposed singular interest in her. "You left me alone by the pool."

"I left you with my sister." He sounded and looked driven. "Marco wanted to discuss something with me."

"So, go back and talk some more business with him. I don't care." She should be used to it by now. She'd been ignored for her grandfather's business interests all her life, but if Luciano thought she was going to marry a man who did the same thing to her, then he was a fool.

*But it isn't his business interests that have you so on edge,* her inner voice reminded her.

"Clearly you do care." He had that superior-male-dealing-with-a-recalcitrant-female expression on his face. "You are upset."

So, he'd noticed.

"Am I?" She turned back to the cards and saw where she could uncover an ace. She did it. She was even better at solitaire than gin rummy. She'd played a lot of it growing up.

Gentle fingers played softly over the bare skin of her shoulders. "What is it, *tesoro mio?* Are you upset by Zia's kiss? It was nothing, I assure you. All is over between us. She was joking with me."

He sounded so sincere and Hope had this really craven desire to lean back into his touch. "That's not the way it looked to me."

"So, this is about Zia's forwardness?" The masculine complacency in his voice grated on Hope's nerves. He liked the idea of her being jealous, the fiend.

"*This* is about nothing. I felt like coming inside. End of story." Was prevarication becoming a habit?

"And playing a game of cards with an inveterate rake?" The complacency was gone.

"Giuseppe is very nice."

"*Sì.* He kissed your hand and told you that you are beautiful." The fingers on her shoulders were tense now, but they weren't hurting her. "You liked this."

If he had sounded angry, she might have remained defiant, but he didn't. He sounded confused and disappointed. In her.

"I'd rather you did it," she admitted. Darn that champagne anyway. The next thing she knew she would be telling him she loved him.

He pulled her up from the chair and around to face her. She kept her eyes focused on the hair-covered bronzed skin of his chest rather than looking up. It was damaging to her breathing pattern, but better for her pride. She didn't want to see his smug reaction to her admission.

He took her smaller hand in his large, dark one. Lifting it toward him and bending at the same time, he touched his lips to the back of her knuckles. "You are very beautiful."

Then he said it in Italian. He also told her she was sweet, the woman he wanted to marry and that her skin tasted like honey.

She was entranced by the litany of praise.

But he did not stop with words. He kissed each of her fingertips with tiny biting kisses, repeating the word *bellisima* after each kiss. Her eyes slid shut as sensation washed over her and then he pulled her into his body, saying something else in Italian. It sounded like, "I knew this would happen," but that made no sense.

She stopped trying to figure it out when he tilted her head up and covered her mouth with his.

The first touch of his lips sliding against hers had the impact of a knockout drug on her willpower.

She'd been starved for the taste of him for days and flicked her tongue out to sample his lips without thought. He groaned and she found herself in his arms, their lips and bodies locked passionately together. It was like that time at his apartment in Athens, but better. She knew what to expect now, what pleasure awaited her in his arms.

She wound her arms around his neck and pulled herself up his body, standing on her very tiptoes, pressing herself as close to him as possible.

He swung her up into his arms, never breaking the kiss. She opened her mouth, inviting him inside and he took the invitation with the power of an invading army. He decimated her every defense and left her helpless against his desire and her own.

He was moving. She didn't care where he was taking her. She just wanted him to keep doing what he was doing, *showing* her he wanted her more than other women. Because he certainly hadn't responded to Zia this way when she'd tricked him into that kiss by the poolside.

Shadows played across Hope's closed eyelids as the sounds of the party faded completely from her hearing. Then there was the sound of a door closing behind them. But still he didn't lift his mouth from hers and she didn't open her eyes. Awash with sensation, her sensory receptors were inundated with pleasure.

The solid feel of a bed beneath her told her he had brought her into a guest room. The feel of his more than solid body on top of hers told her he intended to stay. Her legs instinctively parted, making room for him against her most sensitive flesh. Wearing only their swimsuits, masculine hair covered limbs slid against feminine softness. The sensitive flesh of her inner thighs thrilled to the press of hard, sculpted muscles.

The hands she'd so desperately wanted to touch her were all over her skin, leaving a trail of hot desire in their wake.

She moaned and arched up toward him, pressing her womanhood against his hardness. She trembled. Intimate in a way she could not have imagined, though he was not inside her, she felt possessed. Swollen and hotly lubricated tissues ached to be appeased with a more direct caress.

His mouth broke from hers to trail hot, open-mouthed kisses down her neck and across the skin exposed above the line of her tankini top. "You are no shrimp, *cara*. You are perfect." He pressed his body into hers, sending further sensation sweeping through the core of her. "We are perfect together."

She was breathing too hard to reply, her body on fire for more of his touch, her mind an inferno of erotic thoughts.

"Admit it, Hope. I do not overwhelm you. I excite you."

Did he need the words? Wasn't her body's response enough for him to see that she'd been spouting off earlier?

He rocked into her in an exciting imitation of the mating act.

She arched her pelvis, every sliding contact between his hardness and her sensitized nerve endings sending jolt after jolt of pleasure zinging through her.

He lifted away from her, withdrawing his body from the direct contact she craved.

She gasped, trying to reconnect with his body, but strong hands held her to the bed. "You have this with no other man. *Your body wants me.* Say it."

"Yes," she practically screamed. "You're perfect for me."

It wasn't such an admission. He'd already said she was the perfect size for him, but still, she felt she'd given something away. Admitted to a need that made her vulnerable to him.

Her words had a profound impact on his self-control and without really knowing how it happened, she lost her bikini. He disposed of his black shorts. Then it really was his naked flesh moving against hers.

She cried out with the joy of it and then screamed when his mouth fit itself over one turgid nipple. He suckled and she flew apart, her body straining for a release it had never known.

"Please, Luciano. I can't stand this." She felt like she was going to die, so rapid was her heartbeat, so shallow her breathing. Her muscles locked in painful rigidity as she strained toward him and the pleasure his touches promised.

His hand fondled her intimately, as he had that night in Athens. "You belong to me, *cara.*"

She stared up at him through vision hazed by passion. *"Yes.* But it goes both ways," she managed to pant, needing him to know this was not a one-way street.

He growled his approval as he stroked her in a tortuous pattern against her pleasure spot. Within seconds she was shuddering under him in a fulfillment that both elated and terrified her. Her body truly did not belong to her in that space of time. He owned it with the gratification he gave her, the emotions that pleasure evoked in her.

*"Luciano!"*

He reared up above her, his dark eyes burning with triumph and unslaked desire. Aligning his erect flesh with her pulsing wetness, his jaw went rigid with tension. "I could take you now. *Santo cielo! I want to take you now."*

"Yes." Oh, yes. Now. She wanted to receive him, to take him as primitively as his eyes told her he wanted it to be.

"But I won't." His voice was guttural with feeling, his face tight with strain and sweat beading his temple.

"You won't?" she asked stupidly, finding his denial incomprehensible.

He was literally on the verge of joining their bodies. How could he stop now?

"I do not seduce virgins." His words came out from between gritted teeth, each one a bullet of strained sound.

"But I want you, Luciano."

His forehead dropped against hers, the heat emanating from him baking in its intensity. "I want you also, *piccola mia,* but in a marriage bed."

Her eyes were squeezed shut, her body aching for his possession. "What are you saying?"

"Agree to marry me, Hope, or go home to Boston. I cannot stand this torment of the body any longer." He shivered above her, the tip of his shaft caressing sensitized and swollen flesh.

Then he threw himself on his back away from her, the evidence of his arousal testimony to his words. The fierce grip of his fingers on the bedspread proof of just how close to the edge of control he was.

But it was marriage or nothing. No. Not nothing. Not by a long stretch. He'd fulfilled her. Taken the edge off of her need, giving her the first sexual release of her life, but without marriage, he would take nothing for himself and would not give himself completely.

"Isn't it the woman who is supposed to demand marriage?" It wasn't just a weak attempt at humor. It was also an expression of how bewildering she found her current situation.

He didn't answer.

She supposed he thought he'd said it all.

Maybe he had. She loved him. So much. She wanted him almost as much as she loved him. He wanted her too. She looked at his still erect flesh. *A lot.* He wanted her a lot. He liked her too, had respected her enough to pursue her in the traditional way. Was liking, respect and desire enough?

She sat up, curling her knees into her chest and effecting as much modesty as possible without her clothes on. His hardness had not abated, but his breathing was growing calmer. She looked away, embarrassed by the intimacy of seeing him like this. She wanted to know the miracle of being connected to him in the most personal way any woman could know a man, but she didn't doubt he would stand by his ultimatum.

Marriage, or nothing.

"Luciano," she said tentatively.

"*Sì?*"

"Um…" How did a woman ask this kind of question? "Do you believe in fidelity?"

He sat up and glared at her, supremely unconcerned by his nudity. "Once we are married, there will be no other man."

Was he really that dense? "I meant you. If I marry you, will I have to worry about you taking a mistress?"

"No." There was a rock-solid certainty in his expression that she could not doubt.

"Do you have a mistress now?" She had to ask.

"I told you there was no other woman."

"But some men don't consider wives and mistresses in the same class. They think having one does not preclude having the other." She'd seen it often enough among the rich compatriots of her grandfather and knew that wealthy Italian men were particularly susceptible. Or so it seemed.

"I am not these men. I want no woman but you."

"Always?" she asked, finding it very difficult to believe he wanted to cleave to her for a lifetime and forsake all other women.

He reached out and cupped her cheek. "Always. You will be my wife, the mother of my children. I will not shame you in this way."

Tears pricked her eyes and she blinked them away. "All right," she said, her voice thick with emotion.

"You will marry me?"

She nodded. "Yes."

His thumb rubbed the wetness from under her eye. "You are crying. Tell me why."

"I'm not sure. I'm scared," she admitted to both him and herself. "You don't love me, but you want to marry me."

"And you love me."

Was there any point in denying it? She'd just agreed to become his wife. "Yes."

"I am glad of this, *cara*. You have nothing to fear in giving yourself to me. I will treasure your love."

But not return it.

Was that something so different? She'd practically lived her whole life without being truly loved. Her grandfather had been duty bound to care for her, but until very recently, he hadn't even acted particularly fond of her. At least Luciano really *wanted* her. He could have anyone and he'd chosen her. That had to prove something.

She forced herself to smile. The man she loved wanted to marry her. He wanted to have children with her and he had promised her fidelity. He respected her, he liked her and he desired her, she reminded herself. Perhaps from that, within the intimacy of marriage, love would grow.

"I guess we'd better get dressed," she said, not nearly so complacent as he about their state of undress when she did not have passion to dull her normal thinking process.

He stayed her movement toward the edge of the bed. "I too want an assurance from you."

"What?"

"No more being alone with other men." He was all conquering male.

She sighed. "We were only playing cards, Luciano. You must know it wasn't anything more."

"I know this, but I did not like finding you alone with Giuseppe. He is a womanizer of the first order."

"Well, he was a gentleman with me. He may be a flirt, but I don't think he would go after a woman who was attached to someone else."

Luciano didn't look impressed by her belief. "Promise me."

"You're being ridiculous. What do you want me to do, run from the room if I'm alone and another man comes into it?"

When he looked like he might agree, she glared at him. "That's not going to happen."

"Face it, you were so busy with your *friends,* you didn't even notice I was gone." The memory of Zia's overly warm greeting still rankled. "We had time for me to beat him at gin rummy before you even came looking. I don't think you should complain too loudly about me finding my own entertainment."

"I believed you were with Martina. When she came back to the pool with other friends and without you, I immediately began looking for you."

"I wouldn't have left in the first place if you hadn't let your ex-girlfriend kiss you."

"I did not *let* her kiss me. She just did it."

Hope had to give him that. And he had pulled away very quickly. "You touched her when you wouldn't even put sunscreen on my back," she accused. "When was the last time you kissed my cheeks in greeting? You treat me like the untouchable woman."

His brow rose in mockery. "Do you wonder at this? I touch you and five minutes later, we are naked on a bed together."

"Are you saying you've been avoiding touching me because you want me that much?" It was a novel concept, one that was infinitely good for her feminine ego.

"I promised you I would not seduce you."

And the most casual touching put that promise at risk. At least that was what he was implying. Knowing he was that physically vulnerable to her assuaged some of her fear at marriage to a man who did not love her.

"And now you want a promise I won't spend time alone with other men."

"*Sì.*"

Luciano hadn't liked finding her with David that day in Athens and even less discovering her alone with Giuseppe. She should understand that because she wouldn't like the reverse either. Only she'd made him promise her fidelity. Perhaps he had his own insecurities. The idea was almost laughable, but the strangely intent expression in his eyes was not.

"I won't make a habit of being alone with other men and I will never be unfaithful to you." It was the best she could do, because she wasn't going to go running from a room if a man walked into it and she wasn't going to make a promise she couldn't keep.

He seemed satisfied and nodded. "We will marry in two weeks time."

# CHAPTER EIGHT

"BUT why does he wish to see you before the ceremony? This is not normal." The older woman rang her hands. "*Ai, ai, ai.* American men, they are not rational."

Hope stifled a smile. Her future mother-in-law had very definite views of what constituted proper male and female behavior. Hope's grandfather had confounded her several times over the past two weeks, wanting to approve the wedding dress, insisting on consultation with the chef for the reception and a host of other equally odd, to her mind, requests.

She patted Claudia di Valerio's arm. "It's all right. He just wants to see. He won't touch anything."

Her grandfather had been ecstatic at the news of her upcoming marriage and had flown over immediately to take part in the preparations, much to Luciano's mother's dismay. She was not used to having a man around giving orders in the domestic arena, but Joshua Reynolds wanted to be involved on every level of planning the wedding.

Luciano might be bossy, but he wasn't quite the controller Joshua Reynolds was. When her grandfather was interested in a project, he wanted final sayso over every aspect. For some reason, he'd decided to take an interest in Hope's wedding. Assuming it was part of the strange change in his behavior since the heart attack, Hope dealt with his interference with more equanimity than her future mother-in-law.

116

Claudia rolled her eyes and crossed herself before opening the bedroom door. "Come in, then."

The old man came into the room, his expression as happy as Hope had ever seen it. He stopped in front of her. "You look beautiful, Hope. So much like your grandmother on our wedding day."

She'd never known her grandmother, but it pleased her for her grandfather to make the comparison.

His expression turned regretful. "I neglected her shamefully. Your mother too, but I've learned my lesson. I want better for you. I want you to be happy. Marrying Luciano makes you happy, doesn't it, child?"

"Yes." A little uncertain still about her future, but full of joy at the prospect of spending it with him. "Very happy."

At this both the old man and Claudia beamed with pleasure. For once, they were in one accord.

"Then it was worth it. I did the right thing."

Did he mean sending Luciano to visit her in Athens? She had to agree. "Yes."

He turned to Claudia. "I suppose you have a time-table for this shindig?"

Luciano's mother bristled with annoyance. "It will happen when it happens. I have planned the events, but a wedding cannot be rushed to fit a businessman's schedule."

Surprisingly, Joshua meekly agreed and left the room.

"I think you scared him, Mamma." Martina grinned from the other side of the room where she had been laying out Hope's going away outfit.

"*Ai, ai, ai.* That man. Nothing scares him, but at least he has left us in peace."

Only there was very little of that over the next hour

as the final preparations were made for Hope's walk down the aisle.

It was to be a traditional Sicilian ceremony and celebration to follow. While she looked forward to becoming Luciano's wife, all the pomp and ceremony surrounding the event had numbed her emotions with fatigue. So, when her grandfather escorted her to the front of the church, she was in a haze of anesthetized exhaustion with no room in her foggy brain for fear or last-minute doubts.

And for that she was grateful.

When Joshua placed her hand in Luciano's, a look passed between the two men that she did not understand. There had been an indefinable tension between them since her grandfather's arrival in Italy. She wondered if they had had a business falling-out. She hadn't asked Luciano about it because although he had not gone back to treating her like the untouchable woman, he had made sure they were never alone together.

His hand was warm as it surrounded hers and she pushed her worries about his relationship with her grandfather to the back of her mind.

"So, the pill was not so bitter to swallow, was it?"

Luciano turned slowly at the sound of Joshua Reynolds' voice. The old man looked pleased with himself.

Would he be so happy when his business began to lose important contracts? Luciano did not think so, but he merely raised his brow. "Marriage is for life. It is in my own interests to make the best of taking Hope as my wife."

"You're a shark in business," Joshua said with

satisfaction, "but traditional when it comes to family, aren't you?"

Luciano did not bother to reply. Joshua would have ample opportunity to learn for himself what a shark in business a Sicilian man blackmailed into marriage could be.

The other man did not seem bothered by Luciano's silence. "You won't make the same mistake I did and ignore her. She's a special woman, but I messed up my chance with her. We're not close and we could have been." Regret weighted his voice, making him sound old and tired. "She used to come into my office at home and sit on the rug by my feet playing with her dolls." A faraway look entered Joshua's pale eyes. "I guess she was about six. She'd ask me every night to tuck her in. I was too busy most of the time. She stopped asking."

The old man sighed. "She stopped coming into my office too. I wish I could say she had the love of my housekeeper or a nanny, but I hired for efficiency, not warmth."

The picture he was painting of Hope's childhood was chilling. Having been raised in the warmth of a typical Italian household, if a wealthy one, Luciano shuddered inwardly at the emotional wasteland Hope had been reared in.

"She is very giving." All things considered, that was pretty surprising.

"Takes after her grandmother and mother in that. They were like her. Soft. Caring." Joshua turned his gaze to Hope. "Beautiful too."

"As you say." Watching his new wife smile as she talked to Mamma, he wondered why Joshua had felt the need to blackmail him into marriage with Hope.

"She is sweet and lovely. She would have landed her own husband soon enough. Your measures were not necessary."

Joshua shook his head. "You're wrong. There was only one thing Hope wanted and I got it for her."

Understanding came slowly. "Me."

Joshua turned and looked at Luciano, his expression almost harsh. "You. She wanted you and I was damned determined she was going to have you."

Had she known all along then? Had she told her grandfather she wanted to marry Luciano and then waited for the old man to procure her a husband? Remembering how difficult she had been to catch, he dismissed the idea.

He remembered too how Hope's gaze used to follow him at business dinners and how she had been on New Year's Eve. Luciano was positive that Joshua had witnessed more passion between Hope and Luciano on New Year's Eve than he had ever seen with her and another man. He had drawn his own conclusions about his granddaughter's behavior and acted accordingly.

Hope was not devious, not like her grandfather or her new husband. She was honest and giving as both men had agreed, too soft to be party to something as reprehensible as blackmail. She would be appalled by Joshua's ruthless actions in securing her a husband and equally devastated to know what Luciano planned in retaliation.

He would make sure she never found out.

He didn't want her hurt, but he did want her grandfather to realize the folly of blackmailing Luciano di Valerio.

*    *    *

Hope stood in the bathroom and brushed her hair and then fluffed it around her face for the tenth time. She'd tried pulling it up, but hadn't liked the severity of the effect, besides what woman wore her hair up to go to bed? It hardly seemed conducive to a passionate wedding night, but then neither did her hiding in the bathroom for an hour and a half.

Luciano was waiting out in the suite's bedroom. She'd come into the en suite to get ready on his suggestion. It had seemed like a good idea at the time, but now she was struggling with the courage it took to open that door and join the man she had married. It was the joining part that had her cowering like a ninny in the bathroom.

She should be ready.

They'd come close to making love twice. She'd been naked with him, for Heaven's sake.

None of that seemed to matter to the nerves shaking her equilibrium until she felt like a soda bottle ready to fizz over the side in a bubbly mess.

She wanted Luciano. Desperately. But she was afraid. Afraid she would disappoint him. Afraid it would hurt. Afraid that once they had made love, he would lose interest in her. She was something different in his life, not one of the sophisticated jet-setters he was used to having affairs with. Not like Zia.

She was just Hope. A cultural anachronism. A twenty-three-year-old virgin. Could she maintain his interest once the newness wore off, the uniqueness of making love to a woman of no experience?

A hard tattoo sounded on the door. It had been gentle an hour ago and thirty minutes ago and even fifteen minutes ago, but the impatience he must be feeling was now coming out in the force with which he rapped on the door.

"Hope?" Definitely impatience in his voice.

"Yes?"

"Are you coming out, *cara?*"

She stared at the door as if it might explode into flame at any moment. If it did, she wouldn't have to go through it, she thought a bit hysterically. Of course it didn't and she forced herself to cover the few feet so she could unlock and open the door. She turned the handle and pulled the door toward her.

He stood on the other side, a pair of black silk pajama bottoms slung low on his hips. The rest of his magnificent body was naked.

She swallowed. "Hi." She was making Minnie Mouse impersonations again. That only happened around him.

"You are frightened."

What had been his first clue? The ninety-minute-long sojourn in the bathroom or the death grip she had on the door now? "Maybe a little."

"You have nothing to fear, *tesoro mio,*" he said with supreme confidence, "I will be gentle with you."

Easy for him to say. Not that she doubted his gentleness, but this was different than anything they had shared before. It was premeditated. She found that being overcome with passion was a very different animal to psyching herself up to making love completely for the first time.

If that weren't enough, what they were about to do would have permanent ramifications. The wedding was a ceremony, this was the reality of being married. She was about to become one with this man, a man who inspired both feelings of awe and love in her. But with love came trust, or so she had always believed.

"I'm not afraid of you." Just the situation.

He put one brown hand out toward her. "Then show me, little one. Come to me."

Luciano waited tensely for Hope to come to him. He did not know how much longer he could keep a rein on his desire.

The last few weeks had been interminable.

There at the last, when he had given her the ultimatum: marriage or go home to Boston, he had not even been thinking of making the marriage deal come off. He'd only been thinking of his need to possess her and his commitment not to do so outside the bonds of marriage. He had made a promise to her and the only way to keep that promise was to marry her or send her away.

That his ultimatum had led to the marriage he needed to regain control of the family company caused him satisfaction rather than guilt. He had not intentionally seduced her into marriage. He had kept his promise and courted her and he would be a good husband to her. He would keep his vow of fidelity and she would give him passion and children.

Joshua Reynolds had been right in that at least. The pill was not bitter to swallow, but the water it had gone down with had been rancid. The only way to rid his pride of the aftereffects of the blackmail was to plan a suitable measure of justice for the old man. Luciano did not want to ruin him completely. Joshua was now family, but he would learn a necessary lesson about Sicilian pride.

As Hope took the first step forward, all thoughts of vendettas and lessons faded from Luciano's mind. It filled with the primitive need to mate with his woman.

This woman.

Hope.

Her violet eyes were dark with conflicting emotions. It was the fear that kept him rooted, waiting for her to come to him. She was so beautiful in her cobalt blue silk gown. It swept the floor as she walked and it pleased him she had not opted for the traditional white for their wedding night.

He liked this indication of the fire within her. The hottest part of a flame was blue and when she was in his arms, she burned that hotly.

She stopped two feet away from him. "I'm nervous."

This he had not missed. "There is no need, *carina.*"

"What if I don't satisfy you?" Doubts swirled in her lovely eyes. "I'm not like Zia and the rest. I'm completely without experience."

She said it like she was admitting the gravest sin, but the words had a devastating affect on his libido.

He had to touch her or go mad.

Forcing himself to gentleness, he reached out and put his hands on her shoulders and brushed his thumbs over her collarbones. The fine bones felt fragile under his strength.

"Your innocence is a gift you give me, not a shortcoming you must apologize for." How could he erase the doubts? "I am honored to be your first lover, *cara.*"

She still looked painfully unconvinced.

"I do not want you to be like Zia. It will please me to teach you all I want you to know."

Her eyes widened at that. "Teach me?"

"*Sì.*"

Understanding warmed her eyes. "You like that. In some ways, you're a total throwback, aren't you? You really like the idea of being my first lover."

He didn't deny the charge. He felt primitive with her. "Your only lover."

She nodded. "My only lover." She swayed toward him, her lips soft and inviting. "Then teach me, *caro*. Make me yours."

Her words and the anticipation in her gaze splintered the final thread of his control. He pulled her into his body with less finesse than an oversexed teenager. She didn't seem to mind; her entire body melded to his and her arms came around him in a hold as fierce as his own.

Covering her mouth with his own, he demanded instant entrance. He got it, penetrating her sweet moistness with all the need tormenting him. In the back of his mind was a voice telling him to slow down, to savor her sweetness, but the primal yearning of his body did not listen.

Her tongue shyly dueled with his and small, feminine hands moved to cradle his face while she twisted her satin clad body into him.

Groaning, he swept her up into his arms and marveled at the passion exploding from her small body. She was frightened no longer. It was as if his first touch had dispelled her every concern.

He laid her on the bed and stepped back, his breath coming like an Olympic runner's after the triathlon. *Santo cielo!* She was perfect.

She leaned up on her elbows, the tight points of her nipples making shoals in the material. "Luciano?"

"If we do not slow down, I will hurt you." That knowledge was enough to temper the desire raging in his body.

He would not hurt her. She was too small. Delicate.

He had to be careful.

She sat up and stripped her nightgown down her arms, baring breasts flushed with arousal. Then she extended her hands to him. "Come to me, Luciano. Please."

Was this wild wanton his wife, the sweet little Hope that blushed when he spoke too frankly?

Her pansy eyes were dilated widely; her small body trembled. "I don't want to go slow."

"It is your first time."

"I *know*." She drawled out the word. "And I don't want the chance to get scared again. When you touch me, nothing exists for me but you."

He felt a smile come over his face and suddenly his need for satisfaction was almost wholly sublimated by his desire to show her what it felt to be made love to by a man who knew how to savor a woman.

"You will not be scared, *cara mia*. You will beg me for my possession and I will give it to you only when you want it more than the air that you breathe."

Hope shivered at Luciano's words, her tongue flicking out nervously to wet her lower lip. She was back to feeling fear despite his assurances, or maybe because of them. It was a sensual fear born from the heated expression in his dark brown eyes. Tonight, there would be no stopping.

He leaned down and tasted her lips. "You are sweet, *mi moglie*. Like candy."

*His wife*. She loved the sound of that and her lips clung to his, but he pulled back to sit at the end of the bed.

Her eyes had closed during the kiss, but opened again. He was looking at her feet. "Luciano?"

He lifted her right foot into his hand. "You are very small, Hope."

"And you aren't." His hand swallowed her.

His eyes dared her to imply that was a bad thing while his fingers moved against the sole of her unexpectedly sensitive foot. She didn't feel like laughing though.

She wasn't feeling ticklish, she was feeling excited and more so by the second.

She moaned as he brushed his thumb over her arch. He smiled and did it again. And again. And again. Then lifted the foot to kiss the instep and she moaned again, this time several decibels higher. What was he doing to her?

Feet were not erogenous zones. Were they?

"You smell of wildflowers."

"Bath salts," she panted.

He rubbed his lips along her arch, not kissing so much as caressing. "You're soft like silk."

He flicked his tongue out and licked. Her toes curled and air hissed out of her lungs on a shattered gasp.

"There are over seven thousand nerve endings in your feet."

"R-really?" she asked breathlessly and then cried out as he pressed between two of her toes and she felt the reaction in a totally different part of her body.

He laughed softly. "*Sì*. Really." He touched her gently, but firmly. "If I caress you here, you feel it here."

He brushed the nest of curls between her legs through the slick material of her gown while his other hand massaged her foot. Oh, man, he was right.

She tilted her pelvis upward, desperate for more intimacy, confused by her body's reaction to his not-so-innocent massage. "Yes. Oh… I felt it."

"And do you feel this also, *carina?*"

She bowed completely off the bed as he touched her again. "I feel it! It's…" Her voice trailed off into a gasp of pleasure.

By the time he had given similar treatment to her other foot, she was incoherent with pleasure, having flopped back against the pillows, her body totally open to whatever he wanted to do to her.

Silk slid sensuously against her legs as he pushed her nightgown up inch by slow inch. He trailed his fingertips along her calves, pushing her nightgown up further until his mouth pressed against the skin behind her right knee. He tasted it and the dampness between her legs increased.

Whimpering, she squirmed against the bedspread as he continued his erotic tasting up her legs until he'd pushed her gown into a crumpled mass of blue silk around her waist.

Oh, Heavens. He wasn't going to do that. He couldn't. She couldn't let him. She tried to scoot backward. "You can't kiss me there!"

His response to her frantic efforts to get away was a sexy smile as two big hands clamped firmly to her thighs. Holding them apart when she instinctively tried to close them, he also held her securely in place. "I promise you will like it."

"I..."

Then his mouth was on her. There. She'd read about this, but it felt more intimate than any words could describe. His tongue did things to her that had her body arching toward him, not away. An unbearable pressure built and built inside her.

The pressure burst without warning and her entire body went taut, every single muscle convulsing in rigidity and she screamed. She couldn't hear her scream over the blood rushing in her head, but she could feel the rawness in her throat from the strain.

Luciano wanted to give Hope a surfeit of pleasure, finding vicarious satisfaction in her passion. He could feel each muscular contraction of her virginal body in his inner being. He had never experienced another woman's pleasure so fully as his own and the experience was its own kind of fulfillment.

She shuddered under his ministering mouth, the taste of her growing sweeter with each explosion in her flesh. He didn't stop, pushing her to one higher plateau of ecstasy after another.

Her breath was labored, but then so was his. He felt on the verge of exploding, but he couldn't make himself stop. The sounds of her enjoyment were addictive. Each cry made him feel like the conquering male. Each moan of rapture made his own sex throb with pleasure and desire.

"Luciano, it's too much. Please stop. Please... Please... Please..." She was sobbing with each breath, but still she pressed herself against his mouth.

Her lips said one thing, her body another.

Finally, she went completely limp, little whimpering noises interspersed with each breath and he pulled away, kissing her gently as he did so.

He knelt between her legs and surveyed the effect of the first level of their loving on her. Her small body was flushed with arousal all over, her purple eyes awash with tears, and her mouth parted on shallow pants. Hard, red berries, crested the swollen flesh of her breasts. He reached out and gently touched them.

A moan snaked from her throat.

Her nightgown was still bunched around her waist and he wanted her naked.

Disposing of the silk cloth was easy as she languidly allowed him to move her any way he wanted to. He pushed his own pajama bottoms down his hips, his body experiencing relief at the removal of the light restraint of the fabric.

He wanted to touch only one thing with his hardened shaft, the rich, swollen tissues of her inner woman.

"Are you ready for me, *carina?*"

"I want you to be part of me." The words were a soft whisper, but very certain.

*"Sì."* He would hesitate no longer. He could hesitate no longer. He had to have her.

He covered her body with his in one movement, his hard flesh pressed to the most secret part of her. He had been this way once before, but tonight he would not stop. He would consummate their marriage and perhaps even give her their child. "Now, you become my wife."

# CHAPTER NINE

"YES." It was a broken sound, a mere breath as she curled her fingers into the hair on his chest.

He pressed inward, but though he had brought her to completion many times, she was still tight. "You must relax for me, little one."

"You're so big."

"I am just right for you. Trust me." The urge to press forward without caution and bury himself in her wet heat was almost more than he could bear. "Give me yourself, *mi moglie.*"

"I don't know how," she whispered brokenly.

"Absorb me, sweetness. Open yourself to our joining."

She closed her eyes and took a deep breath and then let it out slowly. Inside, the tight clasp on his body loosened and he slid forward a bit more. He started a rocking motion that made her breath hitch and his body break out in sweat as he went deeper into her.

He felt the barrier of her innocence and would have paused, but she arched up toward him crying his name and suddenly he was sheathed in her softness completely. He stilled immediately.

"Are you all right?"

Her eyes slid open, their pansy depths warm with emotion that caught the breath in his chest.

He made love to her then, forcing himself to go

slow, to build the pleasure in her again until he felt the beginning tremors of her release.

"Now we share it," he cried and gave in to the rapture exploding through him.

Her pleasure prolonged his own until he shook with exhaustion from his release. Unable to hold himself above her any longer, he collapsed on top of her. She made a muffled sound and with the last bit of his strength, he rolled them both so she was on top of him, but they were still connected.

"Now you belong to me."

She rubbed her face against his chest, adjusting herself against his body with a movement that unbelievably teased his recently satisfied flesh. "And you belong to me."

He did not deny it. The bitter pill had turned out sweeter than nectar and he reveled in his possession of a woman so sweet, so passionate and so completely lacking in artifice. She was everything her grandfather was not.

Everything women like Zia could never hope to be.

Tenderness he had never known toward a lover washed over him and he caressed her back, wanting to soothe her to sleep in his arms.

A soft butterfly kiss landed near his left nipple. "I love you, Luciano," she whispered against his skin.

The words did strange things to his insides and he could almost thank Joshua Reynolds for giving him the gift of such a woman.

They spent their honeymoon in Naples. Luciano kept his promise to Hope and took her to Pompeii to visit the ruins of the ancient city. They did other touristy things together, Luciano never once growing impatient with her desire to see and experience new things. He made love to her every night, most mornings and frequently in the afternoon as well.

He was insatiable and she loved it. Shocked by her own capacity for passion, she became a total wanton in his arms. It worried her a little bit, this lack of control she had over her body when he touched her, but his ardor made her feel better about her own.

Every day her love for him grew. Though while she told him frequently of her feelings, he said nothing of his own.

He was solicitous of her needs, tender when he loved her and gentle when she needed him to be. There were several times Hope almost convinced herself that Luciano loved her as she loved him. Although he never said the words, he seemed to like hearing her say them. And he made her feel so special, never letting his gaze slide to other women when they were out, using endearments when he spoke to her, and touching her frequently with affection.

When they returned to Palermo, she was so happy she was sick with it.


"It looks like your marriage to my brother is having a very good effect on you," Martina teased the evening following their return as Hope set up for a billiard shot. "You are positively luminescent with joy."

She grinned at her new sister-in-law. "I'm happy."

Martina laughed, the sound echoing in the cavernous game room. "You two were made for each other."

Hope was beginning to believe that was true both ways and the sense of elation she felt at finally finding her place in the heart of another person knew no bounds. "He's a really incredibly guy."

Martina rolled her eyes. "To each her own, but I think you are biased. Luciano is no better. He couldn't keep his eyes off you all through dinner last night. Mamma had visions of babies dancing through her head. I could tell."

Hope placed her hand over her stomach. It had only been two weeks, but she couldn't help thinking that with all the physical attention she received from Luciano, the odds of pregnancy were good.

But she shrugged, refusing to expose her hidden hopes in case they proved futile. "Who knows?"

The phone rang in the other room and seconds later a maid came into the game room. "*Signora* di Valerio, your grandfather, he wishes to speak to you."

Martina laid down her cue stick. "Take the call in here. I'll go get dressed for dinner."

Hope picked up the phone. "Hello, Grandfather."

He returned her greeting and asked about the honeymoon. She told him about their visit to Pompeii and a garden she had found enchanting.

They had been talking about ten minutes when he asked, "Are you happy then, little Hope?"

"Fizzing with it," she admitted without hesitation.

"That's good to know."

His concern had come late in life, but it still felt nice. "Thank you."

"I finally managed to give you something you really wanted." He cleared his throat in a familiar way that made her realize she missed him even if he hadn't been a big part of her daily life in Boston. "I knew what you did with the coat and my housekeeper told me the car stayed in the garage.''

"I never got around to learning to drive," she said somewhat sheepishly.

He chuckled. "So, that was it." The line went silent for a second. "I don't know you very well."

It was true. He hadn't wanted to, but maybe that had changed. "It's all right."

"Hell no, it's not, but now maybe that will change. I'm damn happy things are working out for you and Luciano. He's a good man. Proud and stubborn, but smart and understands the value of family." His satisfaction rang across the phone lines.

"Yes, he does."

"I trussed him up like a Thanksgiving turkey for you and I'm glad I did." More blatant satisfaction.

The comparison was unfortunate. She couldn't imagine Luciano in such a scenario at all, nor was she sure that a bit of matchmaking could be likened to trussing someone up, but she didn't argue with her grandfather. His matchmaking efforts had brought her and Luciano together.

For that, she could swallow a lot of male self-aggrandizement.

"I guess you did, Grandfather. Thank you," she said warmly.

"I'm just glad you're happy, girl."

"I am." Very, very happy.

"I called to talk to Luciano. Have him call when—"

Luciano's voice cut across her grandfather's. "That won't be necessary, I am here."

He must have picked up another extension.

"Consuella said you were on the phone talking to

Hope while waiting for me to arrive,'' he explained his intrusion into the conversation.

"That's right,'' her grandfather replied, "wanted to talk to my granddaughter and see how you were treating her.''

There was an odd note in her grandfather's voice.

"As she has said, she is happy.'' Luciano's tone was flat and emotionless.

She felt like an intruder on their conversation even though she and her grandfather had been talking first. "I'll let you two talk business,'' Hope interjected.

Her grandfather said goodbye, but Luciano said nothing and she hung up the phone.

Up in their bedroom, she undressed and took a quick shower before pulling on matching lace bra and panties. She was pulling a lavender sheath dress from the closet when Luciano walked into the room.

She laid it on the bed and went over to him, expecting a kiss of greeting, but he sidestepped her. "I need a shower.''

"You look wonderful to me.'' She smiled.

He looked better than wonderful. In his tailored Italian suit that clung lovingly to the well-developed muscles of his thighs, he looked edible.

He didn't return her smile. "Like a Thanksgiving turkey all tied up?'' he asked grimly.

"You heard that?''

"*Sì*. I heard.'' He looked totally unapproachable.

Heard and been seriously upset by it.

"Don't let Grandfather's analogies annoy you.'' She pulled her dress off the hanger and tossed the hanger back onto the bed. "It's just the way he is.''

"He is blunt.''

She smiled again, this time in relief at his understanding. "Right," she said as she pulled the dress over her head. "He's not very tactful, but I think he means well."

She straightened the dress over her hips.

"When it comes to you, his granddaughter, there is no doubt of this."

"You know, I think you're right." It was a novel concept, but one that unraveled some of the pain that had been caused by her grandfather's rejection throughout her growing-up years. "It feels good to be cared about, to tell you the truth."

"Regardless of what form that caring takes?" Luciano asked, his expression just this side of feral.

She didn't know what was wrong with him, but then there were still a lot of things about her husband she did not understand.

"We can't always choose how someone will love us." Or if they would love you at all, she thought. Her grandfather had certainly done a good job of hiding any affection he felt for her before.

"And you will take whatever form of love he gives, or is it that you are happy to reap the advantage of his desire to give it at all?"

Okay, her grandfather's comments had been less than flattering to Luciano, but surely he wasn't offended by the older man's claim at matchmaking. Perhaps his male ego was wounded by the thought of someone interfering in his life like that.

She stepped over to him and laid her hand on his chest. "How we came to be together is not as important as the fact that we are together, is it?"

"For you, I can see that it is not." He swung violently away and stormed into the bathroom.

The door shut with an audible click.

Shocked into immobility, she stared at it for the longest time. What in the world had just happened?

Luciano's reaction to the situation was totally over the top. His fury at the discovery that her grandfather's request he check on her in Athens had been an attempt at matchmaking was disproportionate to the circumstances. Even taking into account that it had been a successful attempt and he might feel somewhat manipulated, was it really so awful?

Luciano was a really smart guy. Hadn't he even suspected ulterior motives when Joshua Reynolds asked for such a personal favor? Especially after that kiss on New Year's Eve.

One thing became glaringly clear to her as she stood in transfixed stupefaction. If Luciano really had loved her, it would not have mattered. His pride would not find such offense in her grandfather's harmless machinations. After all, it wasn't as if Joshua had held a gun to Luciano's head and forced him to marry Hope.

He'd set them up to meet again, but Luciano had been the one to pursue her. He had invited her to come to Palermo, so why was he acting like her grandfather's actions and her acceptance of them was so heinous? If anything was at fault for their marriage, it was Luciano's desire.

Feeling sick, she realized that was all it was. Desire.

And desire was not the soother of pride that love was.

She'd been so sure he was coming to love her, but his reaction tonight showed her how wrong she had been.

*   *   *

Luciano stood under the hot water and cursed until his throat was raw with it.

She had been in on it all along.

This woman he had trusted and believed would make the perfect mother for his children was in reality a scheming witch who did not care how she got what she wanted so long as she got it. Where he had seen innocence, there had been deviousness.

He now saw the initial reticence she had shown to his advances as the ruthlessly manipulative tactic that it was. The classic game of playing hard to get refined to the point of deviousness. She had known he had no choice but to pursue her. Yet, she had made the pursuit difficult, knowing his male instincts to hunt would be aroused. She had done her own part to make sure he was caught in her grandfather's trap.

He had been right to suspect such duplicity and a fool to dismiss the possibility so easily.

The knowledge he had been so used filled him with a desire to do violence. He hit the tiled wall of the shower with his fist, ignoring the pain that arced up his arm.

*He had trusted her.* He had believed she was unlike any woman he had ever known. And she was. She was a better liar. A better cheat. And better at entrapment. Many women had wanted marriage, but she had managed to secure his name on the other side of the marriage certificate. Had she begun making her plans before or after that kiss on New Year's Eve?

No matter what, he was furious at his own gullibility.

The pain of betrayal radiated through him and that made him even angrier. He could not feel betrayed if he had not trusted her and knowing he had trusted unwisely was a direct hit to his pride.

He had allowed himself to care for her, to believe in a future together and all the while she and her grandfather had no doubt been laughing over how easy he had been to dupe. Her feminine arrogance knew no bounds. Telling him that it did not matter how they had come together.

Perhaps that would have been true if she had been a woman worthy of his name and not a lying manipulator.

She wasn't and the fact she had colluded with her grandfather to blackmail him into marriage enraged Luciano.

No longer would he withhold his revenge from her. She would learn right alongside her grandfather that a Sicilian man would not lie down to coercion.

He was a man, not a fool, no matter that he'd been behaving like one for weeks.

Hope cuddled around the pillow in her lonely bed for the third night in a row. Luciano had gone from attentive and loverlike to cold and dismissive in a devastatingly quick and thorough transformation. And all because he was furious her grandfather had played matchmaker.

She'd tried to talk to him about it, but Luciano had refused to listen.

He'd spent the last three days working long hours and although he returned to the family villa before dinner, he did not come to bed until after Hope fell asleep.

Tonight, she was determined to wait up for him, to have it out. She wanted her marriage back. Things had been so good in Naples. She could not accept that something so unimportant could destroy it all.

She threw herself on her back and kicked the covers off. A minute later, she rolled onto her stomach. Thirty agonizing minutes later he had still not come up. Unable to wait another second in the silence of their huge bedroom, she got up. Where was it written that she had to wait meekly in bed for him to show up? She would go to him.

She went in search of her robe. Pulling it on, she left the room. He would probably be working in the study. Light filtering from the cracked doorway indicated she had been right.

She pushed the door open and found him sitting at his desk, papers spread before him.

"Luciano?"

His head lifted and he looked at her with eyes that sliced into her heart with their coldness. "What?"

"We need to talk."

"This is not so. We have nothing to talk about."

She glared at him, fed up with his stupid male ego. "How can you say that? You're being ridiculous about this thing with my grandfather. Can't you see that?"

In a second, he was towering over her, his big body vibrating with rage. "What are you saying to me?"

Okay, so she hadn't been tactful. Her grandfather's bluntness had rubbed off on her, but it was the truth. "We were happy together in Naples. Why do you want to throw that away over something that just doesn't matter?"

"To you it does not matter, but to me it is important."

She reached her hands out in appeal. "I love you,

Luciano. Isn't that more important than an old man's machinations?''

His eyes burned her with a contempt she didn't understand, but that hurt her horribly.

"Do not speak to me of love again. I can do without the kind of love a woman like you feels."

"A woman like me?" What did he mean? "You told me you would treasure my love." Whatever kind of woman she was.

"A man will say anything when his libido is involved."

"I don't believe that." He couldn't mean it. "You wanted to marry me. You said you wanted me to be the mother of your children." He had to care a little, even if he didn't love her.

He scowled at her. "I have no choice about that, do I?"

Did he mean because like her, he thought she was already pregnant? "I don't know," she said honestly. Her menses weren't due for another week.

His laugh was harsh. "For a man with family pride, it is no choice."

"You feel like you have to get me pregnant?" She felt further and further out of her depth, while the pain of his rejection went deeper and deeper.

"Enough of this playacting. You know the alternative is untenable for me."

"I only know that three days ago I was happier than I have ever been in my life and now I'm miserable." Tears clogged the back of her throat and she couldn't go on.

Something twitched in his face, but he turned away from her. "Go back to bed, Hope."

"I don't want to go back without you." Her pride

was in tatters around her, but she was desperate to get through to him.

"I'm not in the mood for sex right now."

For a hopelessly oversexed guy like her husband, that statement was the final blow to her rapidly toppling confidence.

"Neither am I," she whispered from a tight throat as she turned to leave the room. She had never wanted just sex with him and clearly even that wasn't on offer.

He let her go without a word.

The next day, Luciano took off for a business trip abroad and Hope did her best to hide her despair from his mother and sister. She wasn't entirely successful, but both women assumed her melancholy was due to Luciano's absence and she did not disabuse them of the notion. In a way it was the truth. She did miss him, but she had missed him before he left and had no faith his return would decrease that one iota.

On the third day of his absence he called to tell her he would be gone another week. While he had not been overly warm on the phone, the fact he had called at all led to a rise in her spirits. His rejection had not diminished her love or need for him any more than years of her grandfather's neglect had exorcised the old man from her heart.

Was she destined to spend her whole life loving, but never receiving love?

Luciano walked into the bedroom he shared with Hope without turning on a light. He had been gone for ten days and he'd missed his wife. He hated the knowledge. It made him crazy. He shouldn't miss a woman who had deceived him so ruthlessly, but he had.

He woke in the night, reaching for her body and she was not there. He had dreamed about her and ached for the release he found in her sweet flesh. That, at least, he would no longer deny himself.

He reasoned that he had to make her pregnant so his control of his family's company would be assured. Which meant he had to make love to her. Besides sleeping in separate beds was not an option. His mother and sister would notice and his pride would take another lashing.

He'd told himself that was why he called her so frequently when he was gone. It would look odd if he called his mother more frequently than his wife and he had no intention of telling his family how he had been blackmailed into marriage.

He stripped off his clothes and climbed into the bed. His wife's small body was wrapped around a pillow. She looked so damn innocent, completely incapable of the duplicity he knew she harbored within her. She also looked desirable like no other woman did to him now.

He caressed her in a way he had learned aroused her and she moaned his name in her sleep. A shaft of pain went through him. At least she had been honest about that.

She did want him.

He pulled the pillow from her arms and kissed her in one movement. Her lips responded even though her body remained limp from sleep. He tugged at her bottom lip with his teeth and she opened her mouth. She tasted so sweet, it was impossible to keep reminding himself that she was his enemy.

Right now, she was just his wife.

He slid the thin strap of her nightgown off her shoulder, exposing one pouting breast. Caressing the velvet flesh of her nipple with his palm, he nuzzled her neck, taking in the scent of wildflowers that he associated so completely with her.

The soft bud below his palm hardened and she moaned.

His body responded predictably.

It had been almost two weeks since he had lost himself in the sweetness of her body. Thirteen days too long. He ached with hunger for her, with the need to feel her naked skin against him.

She did not wake up as he carefully removed her gown. He laid down beside her again, pulling her body into full contact with his. He closed his eyes, allowing himself to revel in the sensation of holding her again. Something he could not have done if she was awake.

He let his hand trail down her body, brushing tender buds that taunted him with remembered sweetness.

He lightly touched the soft curls at the apex of her thighs and she stirred.

Her breathing changed and he knew she was waking up.

# CHAPTER TEN

HOPE swirled to consciousness, unsure whether she was awake or still dreaming.

Luciano was kissing her, touching her.

She'd dreamed about it so much that she was sure at first it was just another realistic flight of her subconscious and she did not want to wake up to the reality of her marriage and Luciano's absence. She fought her return to consciousness, but it was if his voice was whispering in her ear, telling her he wanted her.

Then his hand made a path between her legs, penetrating moist folds with intimate caresses and she realized she was awake; Luciano was with her; and they were making love.

"You're home," she whispered, her vocal cords thick with sleep.

"*Sì*. I am here, *cara*."

Had he said *cara*? Or was that part of the dream that had meshed with reality?

His mouth trailed down her neck, nibbling her skin and making her shiver.

She whispered his name, clutching at his shoulders. "I'm glad you're home."

His fingers did something magical to her feminine flesh.

"I missed you," she panted, her defenses obliterated by his touch and her disorientation in coming awake to it.

146

"I missed this also," he said in a husky voice that sent shivers of need rippling through her.

He wanted her again. Relief mixed with her growing passion in a volatile combination that had her moving restlessly under him, spreading her legs in an age-old invitation. "I want you."

He groaned his approval and took her nipple into his mouth, but he did not move to join their bodies together. He tortured her with bliss, touching her body in ways he knew drove her crazy with desire.

"Please, Luciano. Now." She arched toward him. "Be with me. Please."

He made a sound that sounded as tortured as she felt and joined their bodies with one passionate thrust.

Tender flesh stretched to capacity, but she did not murmur a complaint. She wanted this very thing. Needed it.

He cried out in Italian and then began to move, his body surrounding her, filling her, completing her.

Afterward, he rolled over so she was on top of him, but they were still connected. He was still partially aroused inside her and little jolts of pleasure shot through her every time he moved.

She nuzzled into his neck and kissed wherever her lips landed. "You're not mad at me anymore."

Instead of answering, he gripped her hips and started moving her on his rapidly hardening flesh. Soon, she lost all desire to talk as sensual hunger took over.

This time they reached the pinnacle of pleasure together and their cries of satisfaction mingled in the air around them. When they were finished, he pulled her into his body and fell asleep before she could get answers to the many questions roiling in her mind.

She snuggled closer to him, reveling in the physical contact, needing the affirmation of her place in his life. He'd been desperate for her, but did that mean anything more than he hadn't tired of her physically yet? She could not believe he could touch her so gently and take such care to insure her pleasure and still hate her.

The absence of hatred did not guarantee love, however.

And she needed his love, now more than ever.

She took the masculine hand resting on her hip and pulled it over her to press against her flat stomach. Her menses had not come. She wanted to take a pregnancy test, but she was sure deep inside that she carried Luciano's baby.

Would he be happy?

His mother would be ecstatic, but it wasn't her mother-in-law that Hope wanted to please. It was the man who had made such beautiful love to her, the man now holding her as if she meant something to him, as if he had missed having her in his bed as much as she had missed his presence in the night.

The last two weeks had been horrible and she had vacillated between certainty that marrying Luciano had been the biggest mistake of her life to an irrepressible hope that things could get better, that he would come to care more deeply for her. After that first phone call, he had called every day. She didn't know if it was because he wanted to put a good front on for his family, or if he'd discovered he needed the connection as much as she did. Did it really matter?

Those phone calls had been her lifeline.

They hadn't talked about personal issues, but he hadn't been curt with her either. He always asked how she was doing and showed interest in how she had spent her day. He'd answered her questions about his business, sharing his frustrations and satisfactions depending on how his day had gone.

Would a man who hated being married to her share that kind of meaningful communication with her?

It was a question she'd asked herself at least fifty times a day since he'd gone. No satisfactory answer was forthcoming.

Still, after their recent lovemaking, she had more peace than she'd experienced in days.

The next day, Luciano was gone before she woke up, but since he had woken her to make love around dawn, she wasn't too upset by that fact. The renewal of their physical relationship had gone a long way toward increasing her sense of security in their relationship. So, that evening when Luciano called and said he would not be home for dinner, she took the news with equanimity.

At least he had called.

She ate with Claudia and Martina and spent the rest of the evening teaching her mother-in-law how to play gin rummy after Martina had gone out with friends.

When Hope went to climb into bed, she was in a fairly good mood even though Luciano had still not returned to the villa. Claudia had assured Hope that this was not unusual for her son and had hinted heavily that he would work less when the *bambini* started coming.

She was dozing lightly when she sensed his presence in the bed and woke up. They made love again and just like the night before, Luciano fell asleep without giving her an opportunity to talk about anything important. To be fair, she hadn't tried very hard. She didn't know if she wanted to tell him about her suspicion that she was pregnant. Having proof one way or the other would be better.

That day set the pattern for the ones to follow. If Luciano did return in time for dinner, the hours before sleep would be spent making love. Yet, no matter how many times they made love the night before, he always woke her around dawn to make love again. And just like the first day back, he was always gone to the office before she came awake for the day.

They didn't talk and sometimes she caught him looking at her with a bitterness that shocked her. The look never lasted long and the one time she'd brought it up, he had changed the subject very effectively by seducing her.

She stopped telling him she loved him, even in the throes of passion. Because although he had clearly not rejected her completely as his wife, she felt an important element of their relationship had been lost. His respect for her.

The longer she played the role of lover, but not true wife, the more she felt like nothing more than a body in his bed.

Even his exquisite lovemaking was taking on a bitter aftertaste when he refused to discuss the stalemate their marriage had become.

She couldn't quite get how he could blame her for her grandfather's matchmaking. It didn't jibe with the man she knew Luciano to be. He was ruthless in business, but fair. Taking out his anger over her grandfather's actions on her was anything but. Not to mention that those actions hardly warranted the fury they had sparked in her husband.

If she didn't talk it out soon, she was going to lose respect for herself. She'd been afraid to make waves, to risk another all-out rejection from her husband, but being a body in his bed and nonentity in his life was taking its toll on her sense of self-worth.

She wanted to find out if she really was pregnant before they talked. Perhaps knowledge that she carried his child would give her a better chance of getting through to him.

Using the excuse that she did not want the first time she met her doctor to be during a health crisis, Hope asked Claudia to make an appointment for her with the family doctor. She felt shy about sharing her suspicions with anyone before she talked about it with Luciano. Her mother-in-law appeared to accept Hope's excuse and made an appointment for her early that afternoon.

A couple of hours later, Hope left the doctor's surgery in a daze of emotions.

She was pregnant.

Thinking it was a possibility was very different from knowing it to be a reality, she discovered. She felt both terrified and elated at the prospect of motherhood. She knew she would love her baby with every fiber of her being, but she had never even held a toddler in her arms.

The prospect of living with Luciano's mother had never bothered her, but now Hope saw it as an absolute blessing. She wasn't alone. Claudia would help her learn the ropes of motherhood and Luciano would be there as well. Family was important to him.

Suddenly she couldn't wait to tell him. He was bound to be happy. He wanted children. She knew he did. This finally would stop him from acting like she only existed in the bedroom. A man could not dismiss the mother of his child so easily. Especially a traditional Italian male like Luciano.

She instructed the driver to take her to Luciano's office building.

When she got there, she took the elevator to the top floor without stopping at reception. She barely waited for his secretary to buzz through and tell Luciano she was there.

When Hope walked into his office, he stood up and came around to the front of his desk. "This is a surprise."

She nodded. She hadn't even ever called him at work. Showing up out of the blue was bound to shock him. "I had something I wanted to tell you."

"And it could not wait until I returned to the villa?" he asked with one sardonic brow raised.

"We don't talk when you're home," she said with a tinge of the pained frustration that caused her.

He didn't reply but led her to a chair by the huge plate-glass windows overlooking Palermo's wealthy business section.

He took the chair closest to her own. "Would you like something to eat or drink?"

She shook her head. "I want to talk."

He looked at his watch. "I have a meeting in ten minutes. Perhaps this can wait."

"No."

His expression was not encouraging. "Make it short."

Darn it. This should be special, but he made it impossible, or was that her timing? Maybe she should have waited to tell him at home, but she was here. She might as well finish it. For a second, the words simply would not come.

He moved impatiently and looked pointedly at his watch again.

"I'm pregnant."

He went completely still, the sculpted angles of his face moving into emotionless rigidity. "You are sure of this?"

"I went to see the doctor today."

"And he confirmed your suspicions?"

"Yes." Why wasn't he reacting? He was acting like they were discussing the details of a rather boring business deal.

"I am surprised you didn't do something to prevent conception so early." His black eyes mocked her in a way she did not understand. "I had the distinct impression you were enjoying our physical intimacy."

Did he think they couldn't make love now that she was pregnant? "The doctor said there would be no risk to the baby during normal intimacy."

"You asked. This surprises me. You are still shy about some things."

She blushed under his mocking scrutiny. "He offered the information."

He nodded. "That is a more believable scenario."

She waited for him to say something about how he felt knowing she was carrying his child, but he stood and looked at his watch again. "If that's all?"

She stood too. "Yes, but..."

"But what?"

"Are you glad about the baby?" she blurted out.

"You must know that I have every reason to be pleased that you have conceived so quickly."

Was this the man who had made love to her with such gentleness the night before that she had cried?

"I could do with you saying it." She could do with a lot more, but she would settle for that.

He smiled derisively. "I am happy about the baby. Are you now satisfied? May I return to my business?"

He had managed to say the words she most wanted to hear in a way that caused pain rather than pleasure. Tears burned the back of her eyes as pain radiated from her heart outward. Why her? What had she done to earn this kind of constant rejection from the people that were supposed to care about her?

She jumped to her feet and spun toward the door, not bothering to answer his hurtful question. Obviously his upcoming appointment was much more important to him than his wife or the knowledge he would be a father.

She stumbled toward the door, her vision blurred by tears spilling down her cheeks.

"Hope!"

She ignored him and made top speed for the elevator outside his office suite. Following a pattern set in early childhood, she wanted only to find someplace to be alone where it would be safe for her to grieve in private. That precluded going back to the villa.

She couldn't even stand the thought of getting in the di Valerio limousine and exposing her pain to the chauffeur. She hated the fact that Luciano's secretary had no doubt seen the tears.

She used her mobile phone to call and dismiss the driver, telling him she would find her own way home.

*    *    *

Anger warred with pain in Luciano. He wanted to go after Hope, to hold her and tell her he was thrilled about the baby. The thought of her pregnant with his child was sweet when it should be sour.

He wanted to wipe the look of misery off her face and he despised himself for his weakness.

She had lied to him.

But what was the lie and what was the truth? She had looked so lost, so vulnerable when she told him about the baby and he had forced himself to contain his response.

The woman who had colluded with Joshua Reynolds to trap herself a husband was not vulnerable.

But Hope *had* been vulnerable. And she had been hurting. Was it possible he had misunderstood what he had heard on the phone two weeks ago? His brain rejected the thought as the words replayed themselves in his mind. Yet, he could not reconcile those words with the woman who gave herself so completely when they made love.

She was too generous in her passion to be such a heartless schemer. And yet, what other explanation was there? Joshua Reynolds had blackmailed Luciano and Hope had known about it.

She had said she loved him.

The reminder caused more disquiet in the region of his heart. She hadn't repeated the words since he returned from his business trip abroad, but he could not forget the sweetness of them on her lips when their bodies were intimately joined.

He wanted to hear her say it again, which enraged him. What was the love of a deceitful woman worth?

Nothing.

Only if that were true, then why did the lack of those words weigh on him in the dark of the night? She slept in his arms, but felt separated from him in a way he could not define?

He was not used to feeling like this.

He did not like it.

He did not like the confusion, or the need she engendered in him.

He did not like the way he doubted the wisdom of including Hope in his revenge, his weak desire that she not find out what he had done to hurt her.

He did not like the feeling that his actions had been stupid rather than decisive.

A short buzz alerted him that his next appointment had arrived. Business was much more comfortable than wallowing in conflicting and destructive emotions, so he forced himself to focus on it.

Stepping out into the sunshine from the air-conditioned building, Hope asked herself where she could go. Looking up and down the busy street, she knew she wanted only to get away from the crush of people. An image of the grounds surrounding the di Valerio villa rose in her mind like Valhalla to her ravaged state. She would take a taxi to the grounds and then when she was ready, she could walk home.

Having a plan of action helped calm her churning emotions enough to wipe her tears away and wave down a cab.

She had the driver drop her on the outskirts of the di Valerio estate. Luckily, she remembered the code for the small gate in the far wall. She and Martina had used it once before on an afternoon walk.

Once inside the estate's walls, she walked only far

enough to hide herself in the trees, then sank to the ground. Her back resting against the trunk of one of them, she let the tears fall freely. It hurt so much.

Not only had she made a huge mistake in marrying Luciano, but she was pregnant with his baby. No matter what she wanted from life, she was now inexorably linked to a man who had as much affection for her as the man on the moon. Less even.

The sobs came harder and she cried out her grief over the years of neglect in her grandfather's house followed by marriage to a man destined to treat her the same way.

A long while later, her mobile phone chirped. She had stopped crying, but had not moved from her place against the tree. She dug the phone from her purse. The display identified Valerio Industries as her caller.

Luciano.

She didn't want to talk to him.

She wanted to shoot him, which didn't say much for the gentle nature others were so convinced she possessed.

He had taken the joy of her discovery and turned it to ashes. His rotten attitude was tearing her apart and she knew that tonight there was no way she could lie with him in their bed and pretend nothing had happened.

She could not bear the thought of being just a body and their baby meaning nothing to him.

The phone stopped ringing.

Ten minutes later it rang again.

She refused to answer it.

He kept calling and finally, she turned off the volume on the ringer.

She stood up and dusted off her skirt before starting the walk toward the villa.

It took her twenty minutes because she didn't rush in any way.

A maid saw her approach and went running inside. Seconds later, both Martina and Claudia came rushing toward her.

Claudia was babbling at her in Italian, much too fast for her to understand, but Martina spoke English.

"Where have you been? Luciano is worried sick about you. We all were. What happened to your cell phone? Why didn't you answer? You'd better call him right away. He's ready to call in the authorities."

She couldn't understand why a man who treated her the way her husband had would worry. Surely if she disappeared, he would be off the hook for a marriage he clearly no longer wanted. Then she remembered the baby. Maybe he cared more about their child than he had let on.

"I'm sorry. I didn't mean to upset anyone. I wanted to take a walk." Which was true as far as it went. "And I turned off the ringer on my mobile." Which was also true, but she neglected to mention she had turned off the ringer after Luciano started calling.

"Why would you turn off your ringer?" Claudia demanded in heavily accented English.

Hope felt really badly for upsetting her mother-in-law so much, but she wasn't about to tell her the truth. Hope's problems with Luciano were private and she refused to visit them on the other women.

"You don't even carry a mobile," she said instead.

Claudia grimaced. "I also do not dismiss the driver and disappear for hours."

Hope looked at her watch and realized it had been

three hours since she left Luciano's office and forty-five minutes since the first phone call. "Are you saying you never go shopping or for a walk where you can't be reached?"

Claudia's hands rose in the air. "*Ai, ai, ai.* I see there is no reasoning with you."

Hope said nothing. She didn't want to hurt the older woman, but she couldn't explain her actions without divulging her impasse with Luciano.

"It is nothing more than a storm in a teacup. She went for a walk and time got away from her. Mamma, there is no need for you to keep carrying on."

"Tell your brother this."

Martina grimaced. "No thank you."

"There you see." Claudia crossed her arms and gave both Hope and Martina a baleful look.

The maid came out at that moment, a cordless phone in her hand. "*Signor* di Valerio wishes to speak to his wife."

Hope looked at the phone with as much enthusiasm as she might feel for a plateful of spoiled fish.

"Hope?" Claudia asked, her expression now concerned.

Hope put her hand out for the offending phone.

Claudia stopped her from lifting it to her ear. "Every marriage goes through growing pains in the beginning, child. Do not be too hard on my son, whatever he has done. A woman must be strong enough to forgive."

Hope forced herself to smile and say, "Thank you."

Her mother-in-law and Martina showed a great deal of tact by leaving her to speak to Luciano in privacy.

She lifted the phone to her ear. "What?"

"That is no way to greet your husband."

The censure infuriated her. "Go to hell, Luciano."

His indrawn breath told her he hadn't liked hearing that.

She didn't care. Not anymore, she told herself. "I don't want to talk to you."

His sigh was audible through the phone lines. "The driver said you dismissed him. How did you get home?"

"What do you care?"

"You were upset when you left my office."

"And this surprises you?" she asked scathingly.

"No." He sounded odd. "How did you get home?" he repeated.

"I took a cab and I went for a walk. I turned the ringer volume down on my mobile after you called. Any more questions?"

"No."

"If that is all…" she said, reversing the roles they had played in his office.

Again the sigh. "I'm flying to Rome and will be gone overnight. I realize it is not the best time for me to leave, but it cannot be helped."

"Why are you bothering to tell me?" She stared across the swimming pool, her body aching from the pain filling her heart. "I'm just a body in your bed. I'm not your wife. You don't even want our baby." She was crying again and hated him for hearing the choking sobs she could not hide.

"Hope—"

She hung up the phone before he could say whatever it was he had meant to say. All his words hurt her and she was so tired of being hurt.

# CHAPTER ELEVEN

LUCIANO called again that evening from Rome. She came to the phone, feeling subdued and just plain not up to arguing with his mother or sister about taking the call.

"Hello, Luciano. Was there something you wanted?" she asked in a voice that sounded dead to her own ears.

"*Sì*, Hope, I want many things, but I called to apologize for my behavior when you told me about the baby." He sounded tired. "I want our *bambino, cara.* I am sorry I was less than enthusiastic when you told me."

She dismissed the apology as too little, too late. Perhaps if he hadn't been treating her so hurtfully for days beforehand, it would have been enough. "Don't call me *cara*. It means beloved and you don't love me. I don't ever want you to use that word with me again."

"Hope, I..." He hesitated.

Strange to hear her super-confident husband hesitant.

"If that's all, I'm tired and want to go to bed."

"I want to go to bed also, but with you, not in solitude."

For once his sexy voice had no affect on her whatsoever. "I don't want to sleep with you anymore."

He said something low and forceful. "You are not leaving my bed."

"Really? How are you going to stop me?" she asked with little more interest than she had felt for the rest of the conversation.

"*Santo cielo.* You are my wife. You sleep in my bed."

"I don't like you anymore, Luciano." She didn't say she didn't love him because it was not true. She did, more fool her. And it hurt.

"*Cara—*"

"Please, Luciano. I don't want to talk anymore. I don't know why you married me, but I can see now it was a huge mistake."

"You know why I married you."

For sex?

He went on when she remained silent. "Even so, it was not a mistake. We can make our marriage work. We will talk when I return from Rome."

He wanted to make their marriage work now? "I can't deal with this. You just keep hurting me and I don't want it anymore."

"That is over. I will not hurt you again, *cara.*"

Was there something significant about the fact that he kept calling her *beloved* even after she had asked him not to? It was such a tantalizing thought that she rejected it immediately.

She had believed too many times things would work out only to discover they would not.

"We'll talk when you get back," she said, repeating his words.

What form that discussion would take she did not know.

When the maid brought her the phone the next morning, she was in a stronger frame of mind and prepared to discuss her marriage with Luciano. He had said he wanted to make their marriage work and he had apologized for being such a toad when she told him about the baby. Men like Luciano didn't say sorry easily and if he was willing to work on their marriage, she was too.

Only her caller wasn't Luciano. It was her grandfather.

"What the hell is going on over there?" he demanded in a voice that had her pulling the phone a few inches from her ear.

"I'm not sure what you mean," she hedged, wondering if Luciano had called him after she'd hung up the night before.

"I've got two society columns in front of me. They've both got pictures of your husband eating dinner with a woman in a swank New York restaurant. That woman is not you."

Hope felt the words like multiple body blows. Luciano had promised. *No mistresses.* But he'd also promised to treasure her love and he'd broken that one. "I don't know what you're talking about," she answered truthfully.

"Could be his secretary I guess, but where were you when he was having these business dinners?"

"Here, in Palermo. Luciano flew to New York right after we returned from our honeymoon." And he'd been furious with her when he left.

Would that fury have translated into actions that would destroy their marriage?

Yet, the idea of a series of business dinners was not so far-fetched. She knew what his secretary looked like after visiting his office yesterday, but if she asked her grandfather to fax the articles he would know she was worried. Maybe it was stupid, but her pride forbore her airing her marital troubles to either her family or Luciano's.

"What else would it be besides a business dinner?" She forced a laugh. "Surely you aren't implying that Luciano would have sought other feminine companionship so soon after our marriage."

"Stranger things have happened, girl."

"Not with a man like Luciano." Until the last two weeks, she would have sworn she could trust him with her life and everything in between.

"There are things you don't know."

Dread snaked through her at her grandfather's tone. "What do you mean?"

"That's not important. Ask Luciano about these pictures, Hope. Communication is important to a healthy marriage."

Coming from her grandfather, who considered asking if she wanted more wine at dinner a foray into personal conversation, that was laughable. Only she didn't feel like laughing.

She rang off and went in search of a computer with Internet access. She found one in Luciano's study. He didn't have a password on the Internet browser, so she was able to go right in. It took her less than thirty minutes to find the newspaper stories her grandfather had mentioned. They were both small articles in the society section of a New York paper.

They mentioned Luciano's name, but failed to identify his companion.

She didn't need the information supplied to her.

The dark, exotic beauty was very familiar to Hope. The woman in the photos was Zia Merone and she was not wearing the expression of a woman discussing business.

Hope barely made it to the bathroom before she was sick.

Fifteen minutes later, she was in their bedroom with the door shut and a copy of the articles clutched in one hand, dialing his mobile phone with the other. She needed to talk to Luciano, to hear a rational explanation for his dinner dates with Zia. Or to hear from his own mouth that he had broken this promise too. Could she trust him not to lie to her? She just didn't know.

It rang three times before being picked up.

*"Ciao."*

Zia? Zia had answered Luciano's cell phone.

Hope's stomach did another somersault. "Ms. Merone, I would like to speak to my husband."

"This is Hope?" Zia's voice rose in surprise.

"Yes. Where is Luciano?"

"He is in the shower."

Hope gasped, feeling ripped in two by the answer. "I'm surprised you aren't with him. He likes sex in the shower." The crude sarcasm just slipped out, but even if it wounded Zia, it hurt Hope more.

"I was not in the mood." Far from sounding wounded, Zia's voice was laced with innuendo.

The tacit agreement to her fears made Hope's knees give way and she sank onto the side of the bed. "Are you saying you spent the night with my husband?" Her voice trembled, but she couldn't help it. She wanted to die.

"Are you sure you want me to answer that question?"

"No," Hope whispered, her vocal cords too constricted for normal conversation, "but I need you to."

Zia hesitated. When she spoke, her voice had changed, become more tentative. "Perhaps you had better discuss this with Luciano."

Hope didn't answer. She just held the phone to her ear and stared at the far wall of the room she shared with Luciano. Was this what death felt like? Your whole body going numb and your emotions imploding until there was nothing left?

Another voice intruded on her blanked out mental state. "Hope? Is that you, *cara?*"

And she realized she wasn't numb.

"Don't call me that you bastard!" She'd gone from whispering to screaming so loud she strained her throat. "You lied to me." A sob snaked out and she covered the mouthpiece so he wouldn't hear it.

He started to speak, but she plowed over him. "You p-promised. No mistresses. I *believed* you. What an idiot I am. Look how good you've been at keeping your promises. You said you would treasure my love too, but you stomped all over it. *I hate you.*" And at that moment she meant it.

"Hope, *mi moglie,* it is not what you are thinking!"

She would be a fool to believe the desperation that seemed to infuse his voice. She heard him ask Zia what she had said. Hope couldn't hear Zia's answer and she didn't want to. She did hear the Italian curses erupt from her husband's throat when Zia stopped speaking.

"Did you sleep with Zia?" she demanded in a voice raw from pain.

"No!"

"No, I don't suppose you did. I'm sure there was very little sleeping involved."

"Stop this. You are upsetting yourself for nothing."

He called adultery nothing? "Were your dinners with her in New York nothing too, Luciano?"

Silence greeted that.

"Maybe you didn't think I would find out?"

"How *did* you find out about them?"

"My grandfather."

"Damned interfering old man."

"Don't blame him for showing me what a lying swine you are." How dared he try to foist the culpability for this awful situation onto someone else? "If you hadn't broken your promise to me, there would have been nothing for him to interfere over."

"I have not lied to you. I have broken no promises either." He didn't deny being a swine.

She'd like to know how he justified that statement to himself. "You were in the shower when I called, Luciano."

"This is proof of nothing."

"It proves you're in a hotel room with another woman." Let him try to deny it.

"I am not."

Getting ready to blast him, she remembered his preference for not staying at hotels and she choked on a bitter laugh. "You brought her to the company apartment? How brazen, *Signor* di Valerio, but then I suppose she's been there before."

"No, Hope. It is not like that." He sounded like she felt, miserable. She couldn't trust what she heard in his voice though, not when his actions had already spoken so loudly.

"It is exactly like that. Zia said as much."

"What Zia said, it was a mistake."

"Our marriage was the real mistake."

"No! *Amore mia.* That was not an error. Our marriage was meant to be. You must listen."

"Why? So you can tell me more lies?" She was choking on her pain. "Your girlfriend was honest at least."

He said something to Zia and then the other woman came on the line. "Hope, I am sorry I implied I slept with your husband. *I did not,*" she said sounding distressed, *"you must believe me about this."*

"That's why you're there when he's taking a shower." Hope wasn't that gullible.

"I am truly sorry I made this sound like an intimacy. It was not. Luciano was still asleep when I arrived this morning to discuss some business."

"Oh, please…" He never slept late.

Zia made an impatient sound. "He was recovering from a hangover, I think. He looked terrible." She paused. "He does not look any better now."

Luciano drinking to excess? Not likely. "You expect me to believe he got drunk, passed out and didn't wake up until you got there this morning?"

"*Sì.* Believe, for it is the truth. Your husband cares for you. I am sorry for the part I have played, but it was only a part. Luciano wants no woman but you."

Hope didn't understand Zia's remarks about playing a part, but she no longer believed the fairy tale that Luciano wanted only her. "What kind of business do you have with my husband?"

Why was she bothering to ask? The answer was devastating to her self-awareness. *Because she wanted to believe. Idiot,* she castigated herself.

"He is investing money for me. A model's career is not a long one. It is nothing more. I promise you."

"You were with him in New York."

"No. I had a show. Our meeting was happenstance, nothing more."

"That nothing resulted in two dinner dates."

"Dinner between old friends. That is all. Not dates. Have you never had an evening with a man that consisted of innocent conversation only?"

All Hope's dates ended innocently, except those with Luciano. "I don't have your sophistication." Her voice should have frozen the phone lines, it was so arctic.

Zia sighed, proving it had not. "Nothing happened between Luciano and I. He does not even kiss my cheek in greeting now."

Hope wanted so desperately to believe the model's words, but would that be opening herself up for further heartache?

"Hope?" It was Luciano.

She opened her mouth to speak, but nothing came out.

"Are you there, *cara?*"

Beloved. She wasn't loved by him, but she was his wife. Presumably that fact had finally sunk in with some meaning. "I'm here."

"I will be home as soon as I can get a takeoff time at the airport for my jet."

"And?"

"We need to talk. Wait for me at the villa."

Was she willing to give him this chance?

"Please, *cara.*"

The humble plea got to her.

"I'll be here."

\* \* \*

Barefoot and wearing a pair of cotton crop pants and T-shirt, Hope flipped through the baby magazine she had picked up in the doctor's office the day before. Her clothes and lack of makeup were in defiance to her husband's ego and her own emotions. As promised, she was waiting for Luciano, but she refused to gild the lily for this confrontation.

She tucked her feet up on the small sofa in the outer room of her and Luciano's suite. At least they would have privacy here for their discussion. Living with his family necessitated eating most meals with company however, having the private *sala* meant there was a certain measure of independence within the confines of the household.

Hope needed that. Although she loved both Claudia and Martina, she had spent too much of her life alone to easily adjust to the continuous company of others.

"Hope…"

The magazine slid from her fingers and she barely caught it before it fell to the floor. So much for a cool reception at his arrival. Picking the periodical up, she laid it neatly on the small table in front her. She fiddled with it, attempting to get it perfectly perpendicular to the edge. She didn't want to look at her gorgeous husband. It would hurt.

To see him and experience the deepest sort of love imaginable and know it was not returned was beyond her emotional capabilities at the moment.

One brown hand covered hers where it fiddled with the corner of the magazine. "*Cara.*"

He was on his knees beside her, the warmth of his hand a seductive lure when she felt chilled to her soul.

Having no choice if she did not want to come off

the coward, she lifted her head and took in the superficial details of his appearance. He had removed his suit jacket and tie and the top few buttons of his shirt were undone. His hair looked like he'd run his fingers through it…several times. And there was an intensity in the brown depths of his eyes she dared not trust.

"Your mother and Martina have gone shopping in Palermo. They invited me to go along, but I told you I would wait here." It was inane chatter, but safer than the questions screaming through her mind.

His jaw tightened. "I'm glad you stayed."

She nodded. "You said we needed to talk."

"*Sì.*" He stood up and swung away from her. "I want our marriage to last."

"Why?" After all this, she needed concrete answers.

"I am Sicilian. I do not believe in divorce." He still hadn't turned around and she was glad.

His words were a death knell to the hopes she had tried so hard not to nurse.

"Why did you marry me if you don't love me?" She just could not believe he was so determined not to have an affair with a virgin that he had chosen to marry a woman he had so little feeling for.

He spun back to face her, his expression almost scary. "You know why. I have been unkind, I admit this, but you must also admit that you carry some of the blame for that."

"Because I was a virgin?"

"Do not play games." His hands clenched at his sides. "I heard you tell your grandfather thank-you for his manipulations on your behalf."

She stared at him, as at sea about this whole thing

as she had been when he'd gone off the rails the first time. "I just don't understand why you're so upset about a little matchmaking. You didn't have to succumb."

"Is that what you call it, matchmaking? How innocent that sounds, but I call it blackmail."

*There are things you don't know.* Her grandfather's words echoed in her mind. "Are you saying my grandfather blackmailed you into marrying me?"

Impossible. That sort of thing just didn't happen in the twenty-first century. It was positively Machiavellian and that kind of business had gone out with the Middle Ages, at least when it came to marriage bargains and the like.

But Luciano's expression denied her naive certainty. "Are *you* attempting to convince me you did not know?"

She glared at him, anger and resentment boiling in a cauldron inside her that was ready to explode all over him. She jumped up and faced him, fury making her body rigid. "I don't have to convince you of anything." He was the one who'd been caught taking a shower while his former girlfriend lounged around answering his cell phone. "If you won't tell me, I'll call my grandfather and ask him."

She turned to do just that, but his words stopped her.

"Do not go. I will tell you." Luciano's olive complexion had gone gray. "You thought your grandfather tried to get us together, but you did not realize the methods he used?"

The methods had been pretty obvious, or at least she had thought so at the time. "He sent you to check on me in Athens."

"He sent me, *sì*, but not to check on you. I was under duress to convince you of marriage."

That explained so much.

Luciano looked sick and she could imagine why. A proud man like him would have been severely bothered by the fact that he was being manipulated by someone else. Her grandfather's weapon of blackmail must have been a good one.

"What did he use as leverage?" she asked.

"Di Valerio Shipping."

"Your great-grandfather's company?" Luciano had told her about the modest shipping company during one of their discussions at a business dinner.

She had thought he was sweetly sentimental for holding on to it when it was such a small concern compared to his other holdings. "I don't understand how my grandfather could threaten it. It's a family held company."

"It was, but my uncle gambles. He lost a lot of money and rather than swallow his pride and ask me for it, he sold his shares in the family company to your grandfather."

"So?" She still didn't get how that could impact her husband. He was the head of the company. Her grandfather could play pesky-fly-in-the-ointment, but that wouldn't be enough to force Luciano into doing something he didn't want to.

"Joshua also was able to secure enough shares and proxies from family members no longer close to the company to take control. He threatened to approve a merger with our chief competitor, a merger that would result in the disappearance of the di Valerio name."

And his Sicilian pride had found that untenable.

"What were the terms?" she asked, a little awed by her grandfather's ruthlessness.

As Luciano outlined the terms for their marriage arrangement, she went cold to the depths of her being.

"So you planned to make me pregnant and then ditch me."

It made sense. Once she had his baby, he had control of his company back and he didn't need her. Even if she divorced him, he retained control of the company through the child. It also explained his chilly reaction to her announcement of the pregnancy. He needed the baby, but Luciano couldn't work up any enthusiasm for having a child with her, the granddaughter of the man who had blackmailed him and so severely offended his Sicilian pride.

"That's why you made that crack about me not using anything and getting pregnant so fast." She couldn't breathe, but she had to force the words out anyway. "You had no intention of returning to my bed after I conceived."

"It was not like that."

"It was just like that! You said so." She sank back onto the small couch, feeling drained.

Luciano came toward her, but something in her look must have gotten to him because he stopped before reaching her. "At first, I believed you did not know. I intended our marriage to be real and forever. You were innocent." He swung his hand out in an arc to punctuate the words. "To include you in a vendetta against your grandfather would have been wrong. This is what I told myself."

His eyes appealed to her, but her heart was bleeding and she couldn't offer the understanding he sought. "I believed you would make a good wife, an admirable mother," he said, his tone driven.

Two weeks ago those statements would have been compliments, but now they were testament to how lukewarm his feelings were for her. "You decided to make the best of a bad situation."

The muscles in his face clenched. *"Sì."*

"But then you overheard my grandfather and me talking and drew your own conclusions." She felt sick remembering what had been said and how it could have been interpreted.

Her grandfather had a lot to answer for and she intended to hold him accountable, just as soon as she wasn't doing her utmost to control her roiling stomach.

*"Sì."* Luciano did not look too good himself. "Can you not understand how I felt? Your grandfather used my uncle's weakness against me, against the di Valerio family. I could not let that go unchallenged."

"So, you decided to get your revenge by dumping me once I got pregnant."

# CHAPTER TWELVE

IT WAS such a cold thing to do, definitely not something he would have contemplated if he loved her.

He shook his head, if anything looking more grim than he had a moment ago. "That was not my plan."

"What was your plan?" she asked, dreading the answer. Could anything be worse, though?

"I wanted you to believe I had taken a mistress. Zia agreed to help me with this. I intended to shame you into asking for a divorce. The baby did not come into it."

"But how would that have gotten you control back of the company?" Hadn't he said if she divorced him, he only got fifty percent of the shares in the settlement?

"I have purchased all outstanding stock, including that for which your grandfather held proxies. Getting back half of the shares would have fulfilled my pride more than my need. It was part of my vendetta."

"You never intended me to get pregnant." Her hand went in automatic protective gesture over her womb.

He looked haunted. "I did not think of it."

At her look of disbelief, he turned away again and spoke with his back to her. "I went *pazzesco*. Crazy. *Santo cielo!* I was only thinking of how you had played me for a fool. How stupid I had been to trust you."

And his pride, which had already been smarting

from her grandfather's behavior would have been decimated by this turn of events.

"Your carrying my *bambino* did not enter my mind." His broad shoulders were tense with strain. "I wanted to hurt you. I admit this. I wanted to make Joshua pay."

"You succeeded. You should be proud of a job well done." Too well done. So much for bleeding, she felt like her heart was hemorrhaging from the pain.

He turned back, his face set in bleak lines. "I am not proud. I am ashamed and I am sorry."

Every straining line of his body spoke of sincerity, his brown eyes eloquent with his regret.

"I believe you." She sighed, trying to ease the tightness in her chest. She believed that he was sorry, but his apology could not undo the hurt. Repentant, or not, he had married her not because he wanted her, but because he'd been forced to do it. The rejection she felt was shattering.

"I thought you cared about me. I knew it wasn't love, but this thing between you and my grandfather—it's so demeaning. The knowledge that our marriage was the result of an arrangement between you and my grandfather so you could get your company back…" Words failed her for several seconds as she struggled to keep the tears at bay.

Finally, she swallowed. "I never would have suspected anything like that, but it explains so much."

He stepped toward her, his hand extended, "Hope, please, we can make this marriage of ours work."

She reared back, almost falling off the sofa. "Don't come near me. I don't want you touching me." When she remembered how he had blackmailed her into marriage, using his body as the bait, she shuddered.

His expression was that of a jaguar thwarted of its prey.

"I want some time to think. Alone."

He shook his head in sharp negative. "We have both spent enough time alone."

"Whose fault is that?" She slapped the hand away that came within touching distance. "I missed you so much, but you treated me like little more than a whore on tap."

"No!"

"Yes! Since you got back from your trip, you've refused to talk to me, but you've been more than willing to use my body. I have to assume that was part of the revenge plan. Make me feel like a tramp and I would hurt even more, right?"

He looked horror-stricken by her words. "That is not the way it was."

"From where I'm standing, it is. I don't know if I can stay married to you," she whispered painfully.

"I will not allow you to divorce me."

"Contrary to the way both you and my grandfather have been behaving, we are no longer in the Dark Ages. You can't dictate my life's terms to me."

He ran his fingers through his hair in agitation. "I made a mistake, I admit it, but I will rectify it. I promise you this."

"And you are so good at keeping your promises." She couldn't help the dig, but she felt no satisfaction when he winced.

"I did not have sex with Zia."

"The jury is still out on that one."

His revenge plot made sense, even down to only

pretending to have an affair. Breaking his word would not sit well with Luciano, but she wasn't ready to let him off the hook on that one. He'd set himself up, he could squirm.

All that aside, how could he keep his latest promise without love? How could he make it better when his lack of love was what hurt the most?

"I need some time alone," she said again. The tears she'd fought since first looking at him, washed into her eyes. "I want to call my grandfather. I don't understand how he could have done this to me."

Luciano's hand lifted and fell, as if he wanted to touch her but knew she would reject him again. "We will talk again after this?"

She didn't see how they could avoid it. "Yes."

He nodded his head jerkily, his normal confidence for once shaken. "I will leave you to make your call."

He turned to go and she had an insane urge to call him back, but she didn't.

She had meant what she said. She needed time to determine if their marriage could survive its conception.

Luciano walked from the room feeling like a dead man inside. His beautiful wife hated him. It had been in her eyes: hatred, disgust, disappointment. Soft pansy eyes that had once looked on him in love now despised him.

She would talk to her grandfather, discuss the sordid events surrounding their marriage. And what would that accomplish? He hoped that time apart would calm her down enough to discuss their future, but an equally strong possibility was that in speaking to the old man, she would lose whatever vestiges of faith she maintained in their marriage.

Luciano had screwed up so badly. He was not used to messing up and knew his apology had not gone off the way he wanted. He had left so much unsaid. Words he found it impossible to voice, words that expressed emotion he had a difficult time admitting he was even feeling. To admit his feelings made him vulnerable and that was the one thing he abhorred above all others. Vulnerability.

But he would say anything, do anything to keep his wife.

He could not even contemplate the empty black hole he would fall into if she left him.

Hope waited impatiently for her grandfather to answer the phone. It was early morning in Boston, but he was already at work.

His voice came on the line. "Hope?"

"Yes, Grandfather, it's me."

"Did you find out what was going on with Luciano and those dinners in New York?"

"Yes. I know everything now. *Everything*," she reemphasized.

"He told you about the deal?"

"You mean about your blackmailing him into marrying me? Yes, Luciano told me."

Hope swallowed tears while her grandfather cursed.

"How could you do that to me?" she asked.

"I wasn't doing anything to you, girl. I was doing it for you. Only one thing you really wanted. I realized that on New Year's Eve. Luciano di Valerio. You've had a thing for him for years, but I didn't notice until then."

She didn't deny her grandfather's words.

"Figured after the way he kissed you that he wanted you too, but he was going to marry some traditional Sicilian girl and leave you in the cold."

"He was engaged to someone else?" she asked, horrified.

"No, but it was only a matter of time. I baited the trap and he fell into. With the passion between the two of you, I figured propinquity would do the rest."

"But he doesn't love me!"

"Bah! Men like Luciano don't admit to tender emotions. Just ask me. Only told your grandmother one time that I loved her. The day she had our baby girl. It's the way we're made."

Hope felt sorry for her unknown grandmother. Marriage to Joshua Reynolds could not have been easy. "Well, I wanted to marry a man who loved me and was capable of saying so."

"You wanted Luciano."

"Not trussed up like a Thanksgiving turkey! Do you have any idea how humiliated I'm feeling right now? I hurt, Grandfather, all the way to my toes."

"What's that boy done?"

Momentarily disconcerted at having her ultra-alpha husband referred to as a boy, she waited a second to answer. "It's not what he's done. It's what you did. You set me up."

"I set you up all right, I set you up with Luciano."

"You set me up to be rejected by a man whose pride had been stomped on by your ruthless arrangement. You can't force a man like Luciano to do something so personal as get married and expect it all to work out in the end."

"Don't see why not. He had to get married someday. Why not to you?'' Joshua didn't even sound sorry.

''Because he doesn't love me,'' she fairly shouted across the phone lines.

''No reason to yell, missy. I may be old, but I hear just fine. The man wants you and for him, that's probably as close to love as any woman will ever get.''

She curled her knees up to her chest and rested her chin on them. Could her grandfather be right?

''You should not have done it.''

''Hope, you wouldn't take anything else from me.''

''I didn't want anything, just your love.'' That was all she'd ever wanted from the two most important men in her life and the one thing she was destined not to get. ''I've got to go.''

''No, wait, child.''

''What?'' she asked with a lackluster voice.

''I do love you.''

Four words she'd longed to hear since she was five years old and lost both parents. They touched her now, healed some things inside her, but could not soothe the pain from Luciano's rejection and her grandfather's part in it.

''I love you, too,'' she said nevertheless.

He cleared his throat, the sound harsh. ''I never meant to hurt you.''

''I can see that.''

They hung up, her grandfather sounding not quite his normal confident, gruff self.

She decided to take a walk and slipped her feet into a pair of sandals. Once she was beyond the formal gardens surrounding the villa, she let her feet wander where they would.

So many things were tumbling through her mind,

she couldn't hold a single thought for longer than a second.

Luciano had been blackmailed into marrying her. She had no right to hold him, even less chance at securing his love. How could he come to love a woman he associated with the pegging down of his pride?

He'd forgotten about getting her pregnant, but now that she was, he wanted to stay married. She'd been humiliated to realize her marriage was the result of little more than a business arrangement between two powerful men, but this made it worse. For him to stay with her, to want her only for the life she carried inside of her was a total denial of herself as a woman.

Luciano had believed she was part of the plot and felt made a fool of because of it. So he had hurt her. He was sorry now and both he and Zia denied having slept together. Hope believed them. She remembered how sexually hungry Luciano had been his first night back from New York. He was hopelessly oversexed anyway, but that night, he had been desperate for her. That was not the response of a man getting all the sex he wanted from his ex-girlfriend.

Where did Hope's love for him fit into all this? She was pregnant with his child, but was that enough to keep a marriage that was nothing more than an arrangement together?

No.

*But her love and his sincerity might be.*

He was right. They'd spent too much time alone lately. If he was serious about trying, she didn't see that she had much choice because to contemplate life without Luciano was to contemplate a pain she did not want to bear.

She headed back to the house, determined to find Luciano and finish their discussion.

She found him on a lounger by the pool. He hadn't changed clothes and his expression was bleak.

"Luciano."

He looked up.

"We need to talk."

He nodded. "Where?"

He was asking her? "Can we go back to our room? It's the only place we're sure not to be overheard by your mother or Martina when they get back from shopping."

He stood up and took her arm. She didn't fight his touch now and some tension drained from him, not all, but some.

When they reached their small *sala,* he led her to the sofa where he sat and pulled her down beside him.

"What have you decided?"

"Tell me again why you were with Zia."

"I wanted you to believe I was having an affair." He took her hands in his, his grip crushing. "But I swear this is not true. I want no other woman, have not since New Year's Eve."

Was he saying he'd been celibate for six months before his pursuit of her? "No other woman...at all...since then?"

"None," he confirmed.

That meant something, but she wasn't sure what yet.

"You wanted me to think you and Zia were back together because you wanted to get back at my grandfather and me?"

He shook his head. "I was devastated by the belief you had been part of the blackmail scheme. Hurt.

When I hurt, I lash out. I did not think it through, I just did it. By the time I came back from New York, I knew I did not want you to believe I had broken my promise."

"But you neglected to tell Zia, so when I called and she answered, she played it up," Hope guessed.

Luciano nodded, his mouth twisting. "Much to my detriment."

"I want to believe you." She *ached* to believe him.

"But," he prompted.

"You broke your other promise. The one about treasuring my love." She tried to pull her hands away at the painful memory, but he would not let go.

"No, I did not. In my heart, I always treasured your love and when you stopped saying the words, it hurt more than I wanted to admit. I made love to you frequently to assure myself that if nothing else, the passion between us was real and honest. That you wanted me even if you did not love me."

The words sounded so like the way she'd been feeling that she choked on her next question. "So, I wasn't just a convenience you used to assuage your strong sexual appetite?"

Suddenly she found herself on his lap, his arms wrapped tightly around her, his face close to hers. "I never thought of you that way. I was hurting and the only place I could connect with you was in bed."

"We connected pretty often."

His sculpted cheekbones turned dusky. *"Sì."*

"Do you want me to stay only for the baby?"

His face contorted and he buried it in the hollow of her neck. "No. I want you to stay for me. I cannot live without you, *cara.* Do not go away from me."

He punctuated the words with tiny kisses that made her shiver.

"But a marriage without love has little hope of surviving."

His hold was almost bruising now. "I know you have stopped loving me. I deserve it, but I love you, *amore mia*. You are the air that I breathe. The only music my heart wants to hear. The other half of my soul. I will make you love me again. I can do it. You still want me," he said as one hand cupped her breast with its already tight peak.

She turned her head and cupped his face between her palms so she could see into his eyes. "You love me?"

"For a long time. Since before New Year's Eve I think, but to admit it would have been to admit the end of my independence. Fool that I was, I thought that mattered. Without you all the freedom in the world would be a tiny cell in a prison of loneliness."

Her jaw dropped open. She couldn't help it. Not only had he said he loved her, but he'd gotten positively poetic about it. "Those are pretty mushy sentiments."

He shrugged, his Italian nature showing stronger in that moment than she had seen before. Emotion warmed his eyes and his body radiated heat just for her. "I feel mushy about you." He kissed her softly until her lips clung and then gently pulled away. "Tell me you will stay and let me teach you to love me again."

"I'll stay, but I can't let you make me love you."

His expression was devastating and much too painful to witness for her to keep up her teasing.

"I already love you. I will always love you and

therefore you cannot make me do something I already am…doing that is.''

She wasn't sure that made sense, but she didn't care because he looked like dawn was rising in his eyes. ''My beautiful Hope! I love you. I adore you.'' He went into a litany of Italian phrases as he divested both of them of their clothes.

They made love on their bed, both saying words of love and need they had held back before.

When it was over, she cuddled into his side. ''So, I guess this means, you really are fabulously happy about the baby.''

''I am.'' His smile would have melted the polar ice caps.

And just to show her how much, he made love to her again, this time touching her stomach with reverence with his hands and mouth and whispering words of love to the *bambino* growing inside her.

Some time later, she was lying on top of him sweaty and sated. ''Luciano.''

''*Sì, amore mia?*''

''You really do love me?''

He sprang up, tumbling her into his lap and grasping her chin so their eyes met. ''How can you doubt it? I love you more than my own life.''

''It just seems so unreal. You married me because my grandfather forced you into it.'' Would she always remember that?

''He played matchmaker in the most unconventional way, but had I not wanted to be caught, I would not have been.''

She sighed and said nothing.

''It is true. You realize I do not wish to pursue revenge on him now? I am grateful for his interference even if I was too proud to acknowledge it before.''

Could she believe him? Knowing what a shark her husband was capable of being, she shivered a little with relief on her grandfather's behalf. ''I'm glad.''

''To hurt him would hurt you and I will never again do that.''

''Sicilian guilt is stronger than the vendetta.''

He turned very serious. ''Not guilt. Love. This Sicilian's love.''

She so desperately wanted to have faith in his love, but perhaps that was why it was so hard to do so. He had been forced into the marriage. How could he love her like she loved him? ''Grandfather didn't really leave you an out.''

He shook his head. ''You do not believe me, but it is true. I had repurchased most of the stock by the time of our marriage. I did not need half of your shares to control Valerio Shipping.''

''But you said...''

''I told you a plan I hatched in hurt and anger, not the truth of my heart, *cara*. *I did not need the shares.*''

And that truth was burning in his sexy brown eyes.

''You wanted to marry me,'' she said with awe.

''*Sì*. So much, I was in despair you would not believe me about Zia and leave me. I was terrified of losing you.''

The concept of him terrified seemed unbelievable, but the aftereffects lingered in his expression. ''That was before you knew I wasn't part of the blackmail plan.'' Understanding washed over her in a wave and with it came unstoppable love and belief in his love. ''You wanted to make our marriage work believing I had colluded with my grandfather to force you into it.''

That fact had gotten lost in her pain and confusion, but no Sicilian male as strong as Luciano would have come to that point without being very much in love.

''I could not lose you.'' His hold tightened. ''You are the other half of myself. Without you, I am not a man.''

''I love you, Luciano.''

His eyes closed and he breathed deeply as if savoring the words. ''Say it again.''

*''Ti amo,''* she said it in Italian.

His eyes opened, burning into hers with purpose. ''Always.''

''Yes.''

''And I will love you forever. I am going to make you feel like the most loved woman that ever walked the face of the earth.''

As goals went, it was a big one, but he could do it. All he had to do was keep looking at her like he was doing right now.

And she would love him like no other woman could.

Luciano looked into his wife's soft pansy gaze, his precious Hope. Her love was worth more than his pride, more than his company, more than anything else in the world to him and he would never let her forget it.

# REQUEST YOUR FREE BOOKS!

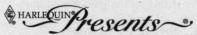

## 2 FREE NOVELS
## PLUS 2
## FREE GIFTS!

---

**YES!** Please send me 2 FREE Harlequin Presents® novels and my 2 FREE gifts. After receiving them, if I don't wish to receive any more books, I can return the shipping statement marked "cancel." If I don't cancel, I will receive 6 brand-new novels every month and be billed just $3.80 per book in the U.S., or $4.47 per book in Canada, plus 25¢ shipping and handling per book and applicable taxes, if any*. That's a savings of close to 15% off the cover price! I understand that accepting the 2 free books and gifts places me under no obligation to buy anything. I can always return a shipment and cancel at any time. Even if I never buy another book from Harlequin, the two free books and gifts are mine to keep forever.

106 HDN EEXK 306 HDN EEXV

| | | |
|---|---|---|
| Name | (PLEASE PRINT) | |
| Address | | Apt. # |
| City | State/Prov. | Zip/Postal Code |

Signature (if under 18, a parent or guardian must sign)

### Mail to the **Harlequin Reader Service**®:
**IN U.S.A.:** P.O. Box 1867, Buffalo, NY 14240-1867
**IN CANADA:** P.O. Box 609, Fort Erie, Ontario L2A 5X3

Not valid to current Harlequin Presents subscribers.

**Want to try two free books from another line?**
**Call 1-800-873-8635 or visit www.morefreebooks.com.**

\* Terms and prices subject to change without notice. NY residents add applicable sales tax. Canadian residents will be charged applicable provincial taxes and GST. This offer is limited to one order per household. All orders subject to approval. Credit or debit balances in a customer's account(s) may be offset by any other outstanding balance owed by or to the customer. Please allow 4 to 6 weeks for delivery.

**Your Privacy:** Harlequin is committed to protecting your privacy. Our Privacy Policy is available online at www.eHarlequin.com or upon request from the Reader Service. From time to time we make our lists of customers available to reputable firms who may have a product or service of interest to you. If you would prefer we not share your name and address, please check here. ☐

HP07

## Coming Next Month

### #2611 ROYALLY BEDDED, REGALLY WEDDED Julia James
*By Royal Command*
Lizzy Mitchell is an ordinary girl, but she has something Prince Rico Renaldi wants: the heir to the throne of his principality! Lizzy is the heir's adoptive mother, and she will do anything to keep her son. Then Rico demands a marriage of convenience....

### #2612 THE SHEIKH'S ENGLISH BRIDE Sharon Kendrick
*The Desert Princes*
When billionaire Xavier de Maistre discovers he could inherit the kingdom of Kharastan, it's a surprise. But more surprising is Laura Cottingham, the lawyer who delivered the news. Xavier wants her, but is she ready to be tamed and tempted by this desert prince?

### #2613 THE ITALIAN BOSS'S SECRETARY MISTRESS Cathy Williams
*Mistress to a Millionaire*
Rose is in love with her gorgeous boss, Gabriel Gessi, but her resolve to forget him crumbles when he demands they work closely together...on a Caribbean island! She knows the sexy Italian is the master of persuasion, and it won't be long before he's added her to his agenda.

### #2614 THE KOUVARIS MARRIAGE Diana Hamilton
*Wedlocked!*
Madeleine is devastated to learn that her gorgeous Greek billionaire husband, Dimitri Kouvaris, only married her to conceive a child! She begs for divorce, but Dimitri is determined to keep Maddie at his side—and in his bed—until she bears the Kouvaris heir.

### #2615 THE PRINCE'S CONVENIENT BRIDE Robyn Donald
*The Royal House of Illyria*
Prince Marco Considine knows he's met his match when he meets model Jacoba Sinclair. But Jacoba has a secret: she is Illyrian, just like Prince Marco, a fact that could endanger her life. Marco seizes a perfect opportunity to protect her—by announcing their engagement!

### #2616 WANTED: MISTRESS AND MOTHER Carol Marinelli
*Ruthless!*
Ruthless barrister Dante Costello hires Matilda Hamilton to help his troubled little girl. An intense attraction flares between them, and Dante decides he will offer Matilda the position of mistress. But what Dante thought was lust turns out to be something far greater.

### #2617 THE SPANIARD'S MARRIAGE DEMAND Maggie Cox
*A Mediterranean Marriage*
Leandro Reyes could have any girl he wanted. Only in the cold light of morning did Isabella realize she was just another notch on his belt. But their passionate night together was to have a lasting consequence Leandro couldn't ignore. His solution: to demand that Isabella marry him!

### #2618 THE CARLOTTA DIAMOND Lee Wilkinson
*Dinner at 8*
Charlotte Christie had no idea that the priceless diamond necklace she wore on her wedding day meant more than she realized. But Simon Farringdon didn't see her innocence until too late. What would happen when Charlotte discovered the Carlotta Diamond was his only motive for marriage?

HPCNM0207